The Secrets of Spirit Energy: Final Conquest

Darius Knight

This is a work of fiction. Names, characters, places, and incidents either are the product of the author's imagination or are used fictitiously. Any resemblance to actual persons, events, or locales is entirely coincidental.

Copyright © 2024 by Darius Knight

All rights reserved. No part of this book may be reproduced or used in any manner without written permission of the copyright owner except for the use of quotations in a book review.

For more information contact: knightvisionstories@gmail.com

First paperback edition March 2024

Book design by Muhammad Kaleem

Artwork by Meta Komik

ISBN 9798851943959 (paperback)

Dedication

To my mom. For years you have shown me what it means to live by faith and to have the courage to believe in yourself. I'm only a strong man because you have always been a strong woman. Thank you for always supporting me and for always having my back. Love you to the end of the universe and back.

Life can be the hand that helps mold us. What matters is the shape we decide to be.

Chapter One:
Going the Distance

In the midst of a raging snowstorm, Desmond is flying with his blue aura on full display. He manages to dodge energy beams that are targeting him. He does spinning and loop maneuvers to throw off his attacker, but even his impressive evasions are not enough.

He aims a fist behind himself to fire off two blind shots. The return fire he got for his efforts shows he didn't hit his attacker.

The assault appears to cease and Desmond wonders if he lost his pursuer. He continues to fly at full speed, but he keeps his awareness open to his environment.

Without any warning, an energy blast is fired from ahead of Desmond that hits him point blank in the face. The attack causes his movements to halt as another blast comes from above that sends him diving toward the ground.

His landing is hard enough to send an enormous amount of snow and ice into the air.

Moments pass before Desmond struggles to his feet. He rubs the back of his head and winces in pain.

His attacker lands mere yards from him with an amused look on his face.

Timulus and Desmond are now standing on an ice cap. They both have their auras present that in turn helps them to resist the harsh subzero temperature.

"Always remember, your power flows within your soul. You have the ability to hone potentially limitless strength, but you must have the will to control it. Look for the fire inside," Timulus says.

Desmond closes his eyes and his aura glows brighter. His mind flashes back to when he ran Whitney through with his sword. He remembers the sadistic grin Czar made when he believed he had broken Desmond.

Timulus looks at him and continues.

"Feel the inferno raging within."

Desmond's aura begins to pulse. His mind once again flashes back to his last battle with Czar. He understands now that the signs of Czar's deceit had been in plain sight, and Desmond knows his anger had rushed his judgement. He remembers when he dealt the killing blow that Czar wanted to happen.

Desmond opens his eyes to look at his right fist.

"Release the pressure!" Timulus shouts.

Desmond's power bursts from his body, but it flows back within him causing his aura to stabilize and calmly surge around him.

Timulus forms two fist and gets into a fighting stance.

"Now show me you're not a waste of my time!"

With amazing speed, they dash at each other and punch one another's fist. This stalemate causes a gust of air to explode from them.

Timulus smirks and uses his Spirit Energy to create a shockwave from his fist that hurls Desmond a few yards away from him.

"After all of these months, you still think too much," Timulus says.

Desmond brushes some snow off himself as he looks up at Timulus.

"What are you talking about? Fighting isn't just a game of muscle. I like to treat a battle like chess and stay ahead of my enemies."

Timulus phases away and reappears behind Desmond.

"Do you still feel ahead of the game?"

Desmond's eyes widen with realization.

Timulus fires an energy blast at Desmond's back that sends him flying upward. Timulus takes flight at a fast pace. He catches up to Desmond and punches him.

The force of the punch sends Desmond plunging deep into the ice cap.

"You can't defeat your opponent with just your brain! A battle should be fought with your mind, body, and soul simultaneously."

Suddenly, Desmond bursts out of the ice cap and flies straight at Timulus in a rage. Once he is close enough, he throws four punches, but Timulus easily dodges them all. Desmond surrounds his fist with a surge of Spirit Energy as he uppercuts.

Timulus dodges the attack and then a vertical gust of energy comes from Desmond's fist that blows past Timulus like the wind.

Desmond smirks as he floats backwards away from him.

Timulus looks very surprised.

"Had I not dodged that, that would've caused some serious damage."

Desmond folds his arms with a mocking grin.

"What makes you think it's over?"

Timulus looks at him with a curious expression.

Out of nowhere, a shadow has cast over Timulus. He looks up to see a big, horizontal wave of Spirit Energy headed towards him. With only little time to react, he strengthens his aura and catches it. Upon contact, electricity surges between his hands and the energy wave.

Desmond smiles as he aims his fist towards the energy wave.

"Still believe I think too much?" Desmond asks.

He fires a blast of energy at the energy wave that triggers an explosion. Timulus is immediately blown away and falls straight to the ground. Desmond lowers himself in front of him.

"I will admit you're right."

Desmond offers his hand to Timulus. He grabs hold and allows Desmond to help him to his feet.

"I need to find a way for my body and mind to work together instead of independently, but in the meantime, I'll stick to what I know."

Timulus smiles warmly at him.

"That style suits you. I must admit Desmond, you had me overwhelmed with that attack. I'm curious, how does it work?"

"Well," Desmond says in a serious tone.

"Remember that gust of energy that flew past you like a breeze? I sent that from my fist and directed it into the air so it could materialize. Then, when I'm ready, I can make it rain down on my target. It can also move in any direction I want it to go and manifest in multiple forms."

Timulus rubs his chin as he considers what Desmond just said.

"So, you were able to make your Spirit Energy form into a gas-like substance and on command, you were able to transmute it into a solid mass?"

Desmond nods his head in agreement.

"Yea, what you said."

"That is very interesting. Outside of what I have been teaching you, there are techniques you've picked up on your own. I now have a better understanding of why Master Berengia has so much faith in you. I believe it's time to return you home. I'm not sure how much more I can teach you."

"I gotta say, Tim, you're not the asshole I thought you'd be. I really appreciate all of this."

"It is part of my duty, and please stop calling me Tim."

"After you drop me off home, don't be a stranger. I'll feel like a cheap hooker if you don't check in every once in a while."

Timulus makes a confused expression.

"What is a hooker? Some type of worn-out device?"

Desmond smirks as he shakes his head.

"You could say that. Let's get out of here, Tim."

Timulus does an aggravated exhale. A flash occurs, and they are gone.

Meanwhile at SAGA Headquarters, Vyncent is in the middle of a training exercise that consists of eight floating circular robots firing lasers at him. Vyncent doesn't have his aura present, but he is successfully dodging every laser that comes his way.

While in the midst of running and dodging, one of the lasers manages to hit him on his leg. He grunts in pain and falls to the ground. All the robots surround him. He looks around at them. He can hear the robots getting ready to fire.

Vyncent tightly clutches his fist with a focused resolve. All the muscles in his body bulge as his aura forms.

One of the robots fires the first shot. He gathers Spirit Energy around his fist and punches the laser in another direction.

He gets up to run, and the other robots begin to shoot at him. His speed greatly increases as he dodges the lasers.

He stops running and prepares for his next move.

He points three fingers forward as his aura glows brighter. The tips of those three fingers glow with an intensified aura, but suddenly the auras begin to dim and flicker a few times before it slowly fades away. His face goes from determined to disappointed in a matter of seconds.

"Crap," Vyncent says as he lowers his hand.

The robots open fire at him. Without hesitation, he dodges five of the lasers and laces his fist with Spirit Energy. He punches the other three lasers, causing them to reverse and destroy two robots on contact.

Vyncent runs full speed for a few feet before jumping into the air. He aims both of his fists to his left and fires an energy blast. The force from it maneuvers him into the air. The two robots below fire but end up destroying each other instead. He aims upward and fires another energy blast to quicken his descent to the ground.

One of the remaining robots approaches him. He destroys it with an energy blast. He smirks as he looks at the smoldering robot, but suddenly he is shot in the back by another robot.

Vyncent falls to one knee as he looks behind himself. The robot fires again, but he drops flat on his back to avoid the laser. After the laser misses, he fires with both fists to destroy it.

He stands up with a smile as he raises his fist into the air.

"You see that?"

A control room is above him with Kelly inside. She leans in to speak into the microphone.

"That was good Vyncent, but what happened when you were building your energy earlier?"

"Well, I was trying to use a special technique, but it didn't work. I still have a hard time with concentrated energy attacks," Vyncent confesses with a sheepish grin.

While they are having this conversation, the last remaining robot is approaching him from behind. Before it has the chance to shoot, a laser from a different direction is fired that destroys it.

Vyncent looks behind himself and sees Karina across the room. Her gauntlet has smoke coming from it. His muscles return to normal as his aura disperses. He chuckles nervously.

"Thanks."

Karina shakes her head as she lowers her gauntlet.

"You need to remember to always be aware of your surroundings, Vyncent. Just because you think you're in the clear doesn't mean you are. Always assume there is danger on the battlefield."

Vyncent looks down at the floor.

"She's right," Kelly says.

Vyncent looks behind himself and sees Kelly at the other end of the room.

"When did you get in here?" Vyncent asks with a puzzled expression.

"Doesn't matter. This is just another example that you still are not taking this as seriously as you should."

Vyncent takes a few steps towards her with an agitated posture.

"You two need to cut me a little slack here. Unlike you, I'm not a trained killer nor do I care to be. I'll agree that some of these exercises could've gone better, but I have shown a great deal of progress in this short amount of time. I need you to trust that I'll be at my best when it counts."

The room is filled with silence as Vyncent looks at them.

Kelly walks up to him and slaps him.

"Your best is needed at all times, Vyncent. If you don't show it now, then how do you expect us to trust that you'll have it when it really matters? You are now one of the most powerful beings on this planet, so excuse me if I expect more out of you. Evil won't take a break, so why should you? You have a responsibility."

Vyncent cuts her off.

"You kidnapped me, remember? I'm sorry if I'm not taking this as seriously as you want. Especially considering this 'responsibility' was forced on me."

Kelly takes another step.

"You agreed to this."

"Waking up strapped to a machine didn't feel like much of a choice. The decision was made for me."

He turns to Karina.

"And you. You have just as much to blame. You lured me into that closet and allowed them to take me. I'm going to help Desmond because he's my friend, and he needs all the help he can get."

He turns back to face Kelly with an icy glare.

"Not because you expect this from me. Make no mistake, Kelly. You may be a very scary lady, but I am not your toy soldier!"

Vyncent rushes out of the room with an angry stride.

After a pregnant silence, Karina sighs and looks at Kelly.

"Maybe we have been too hard on him."

Kelly grunts her agreement, but she doesn't offer anything else. Kelly shifts her eyes to Karina's hands and notices her nails.

Karina's nails have a checkerboard design with two-toned green polish. Kelly wonders when was the last time she ever saw Karina with painted nails, let alone a tailored design.

Weird, Kelly thinks.

Chapter Two:
Discovery

On the outskirts of an isolated area on Seredia Island, there is a private observatory resting on top of a hill. The building itself is dome shaped and houses a complete remake of a Zeiss telescope. There is also a custom built, 120-inch reflecting telescope that sits in the middle of the main room.

The observatory scientist, Doctor Edward Williams, is cross-referencing his Zeiss telescope and another machine that can detect heat signatures. After another glance, he takes a moment to write down some notes with a fearful expression. Then he takes a few steps back while he stares upward with a concerned demeanor.

"What are you worried about, Doctor Williams?" J-Nel asks from across the room.

Doctor Williams flinches in surprise as he turns to look at J-Nel.

"When did you get here?"

Doctor Williams shakes his head and approaches J-Nel while rubbing his eyes with both hands.

"Never mind. When you first hired me to track anomalies on Seredia Island, I initially thought you were a paranoid individual."

J-Nel slides his hands into his pockets.

"And now?"

Doctor Williams looks at him with a serious expression.

"Your paranoia is valid."

Doctor Williams rushes over to a large monitor and pulls up a split screen. On the left is an image that shows a large heat signature. On the right is nothing but the sky with remarkable clouds.

J-Nel takes a few steps toward the monitor and strokes his goatee.

"What exactly am I looking at?"

Doctor Williams smiles.

"I have not the slightest idea. And that's the point."

J-Nel looks at him with disbelief as he mumbles, "Maybe hiring you was a mistake."

"You see these heat signatures here? It indicates a formidable mass that was the size of a small Honda just a few months ago. Now, it rivals the size of a two-story house.

Also, the heat it's generating isn't necessarily heat that machines or bodies produce. The machine I used to detect it is primarily used to find a hot spot of Seredium, and in case you're not aware, Seredium generates its own special kind of heat. No other machine but this one could detect whatever that is.

I'm not convinced this is some sort of space craft either. This is just a guess, mind you, but I think we're looking at a gateway to something. Whatever that thing is, it's resting right below Earth's atmosphere. It may be time to bring her in on this."

J-Nel looks at it carefully before shaking his head.

"No. At least not until I know everyone is ready to deal with this."

"With all due respect, sir, whatever that mass is, it is something this world has never seen. I'm also convinced we may be looking at a portal of some sort."

"If I show them these findings now, fear will drive their next actions and I can't have that. I'd rather they finish their preparations so we can handle this with a clear mind."

Doctor Williams looks at him and back at the monitor.

"I do hope you know what you're doing."

J-Nel fidgets with a metal band on his wrist as he stares at the monitor with a smoldering intensity.

Chapter Three:
Tyrant

    Montezuma has completely taken over Pluto. Most of what was considered civilized has significantly been downgraded to a primitive lifestyle. He now has Plutonian followers under his regime, but those who oppose him have become slaves. His followers dress in armor identical to the design of what used to be Berengia's army.

    All over the planet, he has countless enslaved Plutonians excavating several areas to uncover something he believes is hidden. He is levitating in the air with his red aura present and his eyes closed.

    He thinks, *In case Czar fails me again, I need to find the secret for myself or the next best thing. Somewhere beneath the surface is a cave that will lead me to the legend of Hurak. His power is the key. I'm sure of it. Between trying to find the legend and my other project, I'm starting to feel stressed.*

He opens his eyes and looks down while scratching at the tattoo on his chest.

On the ground level, an explosion occurs that kills a handful of Plutonians. One of Montezuma's generals is dishing out commands.

"If none of you want to die next, then I suggest you move out of the way when I say move!"

The general laughs as he lowers himself to the ground in front of the hole that was created.

Montezuma's eyes widen as he dashes to the ground. He shoves his general out of the way to gaze into the hole himself.

"This is it," Montezuma says quietly.

Inside of the hole is a downward spiraling staircase that leads to a set of large double doors. They are made of gold, but there are no handles to be seen.

Montezuma approaches the doors and places his hand on them as he admires the ancient language they are engraved with.

"Bring me the Elder," he says calmly.

Shortly after his command, two of his Plutonian followers forcefully bring in an older Plutonian and shove him to the ground.

"Can you read this, Elder," Montezuma asks without looking at him.

The Elder Plutonian slowly stands with help from his cane and carefully looks at the double doors.

"That is an ancient language of man. This was here before even my generation. Even if I could understand it, I wouldn't serve you."

Montezuma whips around and grabs the Elder by the throat to lift him into the air.

"Do not test my patience right now, you insect! You may not be able to read this, but you know who can."

Montezuma's eyes glow with Spirit Energy as his grip tightens.

"Somewhere on this planet are a group of sons that were taught the ancient language. Where are they?"

The Elder remains calm under the pressure and refuses to say a word.

Montezuma shifts his eyes and releases the Elder.

The Elder rubs his neck and coughs slightly.

Montezuma looks down on him with a blank expression.

"I realize my methods will not work with you. You are too disciplined to give in to a violent demand. I respect that, but there is always a way to break even the most stubborn of creatures."

The Elder looks at Montezuma with a nervous demeanor.

Without breaking eye contact with the Elder, Montezuma laces his hand with Spirit Energy and reaches out to the side. One of the enslaved Plutonians flies towards Montezuma, and he catches her by the neck. The Plutonian screams and pleads for her life as she squirms.

The Elder looks shocked and fearful now.

"Where are the sons?" Montezuma calmly asks.

The Elder looks at him with wide eyes, but he calms down, looks away, and defiantly shuts his eyes.

The female Plutonian continues to squirm as she pleads for her life.

"Please don't hurt me!"

Montezuma forces her to her knees. His eyes flash and within a fraction of a second, her head explodes.

The Elder looks at her headless body as it flops to the ground. Some of her blood had splashed on his hands and face. He looks on in horror.

The enslaved Plutonians in the area have stopped working and look at Montezuma with great fear as they all scream.

Montezuma looks at the elder and decides to try again.

"Where are the sons?"

The Elder remains silent which causes Montezuma to become aggravated. He opens both hands, and a Plutonian flies into each one. Their heads instantly explode as their bodies drop to the ground. Just as quickly, Montezuma kills two more Plutonians the same way without hesitation and two more after that.

During this bloodshed, all the enslaved Plutonians in the area are screaming in terror. They try to run away, but the general and the Plutonian followers are blocking them from escaping.

The Elder puts his hands on his face before he vomits uncontrollably. He wipes his mouth and staggers, regaining his composure.

"Stop this madness! I know who they are, but they went into hiding once they heard you were looking for the cave. I can show you where to start looking."

The Elder's clothes are drenched with blood. He tries his hardest to wipe the blood from his face and arms, but all he manages to do is smear it. He stares at his hands with such agony and regret from letting so many of his fellow Plutonians die. He looks up at Montezuma with tears in his eyes.

Montezuma is breathing hard as blood is dripping from his hands. He takes a moment to collect himself as he flicks some of the blood off. He looks down at the elder with a slight grin.

"Lead the way.

Chapter Four:
New Players

In the Business sector of Seredia Island, Vyncent is sitting at a bar watching the news on a television.

The bartender walks over and slides him six shots of tequila and a beer. He immediately drinks three of the shots and makes the ugliest face a person can make.

Vyncent looks to his right and notices a woman sitting at the other end with a margarita in front of her as well as four shots of Whiskey.

The woman looks to be about five seven and has a caramel skin complexion, a small golden nose hoop, and hazel eyes. She has dark brown dreads to her shoulders with four small golden bands on the left and right of her head.

She is dressed in a white tank top, a light brown designer jacket, ripped dark blue jeans, and a pair of brown Timberland boots.

She has her phone sitting up on a small stand. She stares at it for a while, then she slams her phone face down, drinks two shots, and gulps half of her margarita. She places her hand on her face as she quietly cries and abruptly drops her head on the counter.

Vyncent looks her up and down just before he forwards his attention back to his own shots.

Vyncent glances behind himself when he hears the doors to the bar open. Three men walk in as if they're looking for someone. All three of them are well built physically with distinct features.

The man on the far left has a pale complexion, blue eyes, shoulder length dark brown hair with blonde highlights, a chiseled jaw, and an unusual scar below his right eye.

The man on the right has a dark brown complexion, a thick frohawk that is eight inches tall, green eyes, and a rather large nose.

The one in the middle is taller than his companions with the muscle to match his stature. He looks as if he is of Asian descent. He has a short, spiky hairstyle and a medium-sized platinum bullnose ring.

Vyncent looks at them again and notices that all three of them are now staring at him.

The three men look at each other as they take a seat at a nearby table.

Vyncent faces forward and downs another one of his shots. As he puts the glass down, the man with the frohawk is sliding onto the stool next to him.

Vyncent stares at him.

"What do you want?"

"You will come with us," the man bluntly says.

Vyncent drinks his last two remaining shots and casually cuts his eyes at him.

"I don't know what your game is, but I honestly don't care. It's bad enough I can't get as drunk as I usually can. I'll give you an opportunity to leave before you get hurt."

The man smirks as he stands up, but he doesn't take his eyes off Vyncent.

"Get up right now, or everyone in this room will die. Including that ugly female you were lusting after before we walked in."

Immediately after his comment, the woman across from them slams her right hand on the counter and glares into their direction. She speaks with a soft African accent.

"I... am not UGLY!"

Due to the alcohol, there is a strong slur in her speech.

"I am... am... beautiful and had my dad not just passed away, he would've stuck up for me and told you that his self."

The woman wipes away her tears as she approaches the man.

"You think you're a big fella, don' chu?"

The man scrunches his nose and tries to move his face away due to the strong smell of alcohol on her breath.

Vyncent slowly gets up to intervene.

"Miss, I think me and these guys will continue this outside. Why don't you order yourself a Sprite and tell the bartender to put your drinks on my tab?"

She shoves the frohawk man out of the way and gets in Vyncent's face.

"Oh! So, you want to be a big fella too, huh? You think I can't buy my own drinks. I'm not a piece of meat!"

She turns to the other guy.

"And I'm not ugly!"

She raises her fist as if she's going to punch him, but she hiccups and immediately falls forward onto the floor.

The man looks at Vyncent with a questioning expression.

"Do all of the females on your planet act in this manner?"

Vyncent shrugs.

Out of nowhere, the woman stands up and wipes the drool from her mouth.

"Where do you think you're going?"

She throws a slow punch at him, but the man simply leans to the side causing her to fall onto a barstool and then back to the floor. She places her hand on the counter to help herself up.

"Had enough yet?"

The man now looks aggravated.

"Enough of this!"

He grabs her by the throat and lifts her into the air.

Everyone in the bar has now forwarded their attention to the scene that has now escalated.

The man squeezes her throat slightly as she grunts in pain.

"Come with us, or I will rip her head from her body."

Vyncent now has both of his hands in fists.

"Fine, but put her down."

"I think I'll bring her along in case you have a change of heart."

The other two guys have gotten up to join the man. He looks Vyncent up and down.

"Lead the way outside."

Vyncent leads them to a side exit of the bar that places them into an alley. Once they are outside, he looks back at them.

"Follow me."

He takes flight. They follow without hesitation.

The frohawk man continues to hold the woman by her throat while flying, but it appears she has lost consciousness.

After a short flight, they arrive in the midst of countless trees of the island's forest.

Vyncent looks at all three of the beings with him.

"What are you?"

The man tosses the woman to the side, but she remains unconscious.

"I am Fraq, leader of this Trijule Squadron."

He looks at the pale man.

"This is Lorit."

Lastly, he looks at the Asian man.

"And this is Miz. He is an outstanding tracker."

Vyncent looks at the woman and then back at the three.

"Since you sought me out, I'm sure you know my name. You still haven't told me what you are."

Simultaneously, they all create royal blue auras around their bodies as their appearances begin to morph.

Their noses, eyebrows, and ears disappear. Their skin changes into a dark silver complexion as their eyes widen and yellow rings form around them.

Fraq's frohawk becomes burgundy, curlier, and wild with five dreadlocks growing out of the back of it.

Lorit's hair thickens and becomes spikier as it grows down to the middle of his back. The color also changes to a bright orange, and the highlights turn dark red.

Miz's head loses all its hair except for the top. His short, spiky hair rises and turns green. The tips of his hair slowly turn dark blue.

Fraq takes a few steps towards Vyncent.

"We are Plutonians. We are part of the front line of Montezuma's regime, and we are here to assist Czar."

Their auras intensify so strongly that their human clothes evaporate to reveal Plutonian armor.

"Will you come quietly or by force?" Fraq asks with a demanding tone.

Vyncent clutches his fist and wind forms around him.

Lorit and Miz take a few steps to be beside their leader. Lorit snickers before speaking.

"I was hoping he would choose the hard way."

Fraq crosses his arms and calmly says, "Take him."

Lorit and Miz charge at Vyncent, but he holds his ground without showing any fear.

Before they get close enough, Vyncent fires an energy blast towards the ground to create a smokescreen from the dirt.

Lorit and Miz immediately stop to shield their eyes.

Suddenly from the dirt cloud, an energy blast hits Lorit dead on, which sends him flying through a few trees.

Vyncent emerges from the cloud and punches at Miz, but he catches Vyncent's fist. Vyncent looks surprised by the grin on Miz's face.

Right, this one is a tracker. He probably can sense an attack coming regardless of his position. So why didn't he try to deflect my energy attack? Vyncent thinks.

Vyncent attempts a spin-kick, but Miz blocks it with his forearm without any effort. Vyncent now looks annoyed and begins to launch a series of punches at him. One by one, Miz is either blocking or redirecting Vyncent's attacks elsewhere.

Vyncent swings an uppercut, but Miz slaps his fist away and sucker punches Vyncent a few yards away.

After landing on his back, Vyncent gets to his feet and wipes the blood from his nose. He looks at Miz who has a smirk on his face and notices Lorit who has recovered from his fall. They are now standing side by side.

Vyncent clutches his fist. His muscles bulge as his aura appears around his body.

Miz's face changes from confident to worried in an instant. Lorit and Miz get into battle position and await Vyncent's next move.

Vyncent positions himself as if he is about to begin a sprint run.

I knew it. By projecting my own unique Spirit Energy, it throws off his natural senses, Vyncent thinks.

Vyncent dashes in their direction. Once Vyncent makes it halfway, Miz charges at him, and Lorit follows soon after.

When he gets close enough, Vyncent bluffs a punch at Miz. Miz immediately brings his hand up to block, but Vyncent retracts and spin-kicks him across his face.

As soon as Miz is knocked out of the way, Lorit punches Vyncent in the stomach, causing his movement to cease.

Vyncent grabs Lorit's arm while intensifying his aura and slams him to the ground face first.

Vyncent notices Miz is coming for him. Miz attacks with a punch, but Vyncent meets Miz's fist with his own.

Lorit places his hands on the ground to thrust his foot upward into Vyncent's chin.

Miz puts Vyncent in a full nelson and Lorit delivers continuous punches to Vyncent's stomach.

After the fifth punch, Vyncent strengthens his aura and hits Miz in the nose with the back of his head causing Miz's hold to loosen. Vyncent uses the opportunity to break free by elbowing him in the stomach.

Vyncent aims a fist at both of them. He fires an energy blast at their faces that knocks them unconscious.

Vyncent is now breathing hard and begins to look around. He looks confused because he does not see the girl anywhere.

"Where is she?" he asks angerily.

He looks at Fraq who looks unconcerned.

"Unlike them, I am fully aware of what you can do. Before we arrived, I urged them to study the potential you possess, but they decided you were the weak link and not to be taken seriously."

The torso of his armor and his wrist begin to glow.

"I will not make their mistake and underestimate you. I have been instructed not to kill you."

Fraq begins to walk toward Vyncent with his hands open.

"I was not told how much of your life had to be intact."

The energy in his wrists glows brighter as a small ball of energy forms in each hand. He makes a fist with both hands to cause the energy to surround his fist. A pair of swords made up of energy forms in his hands. The swords resemble Scimitar blades.

Vyncent strengthens his aura around both of his forearms and stands ready for him.

Fraq runs at Vyncent with incredible speed. He zigzags around Vyncent so fast that Vyncent can hardly see his legs moving.

Vyncent aims his fist towards the ground and fires multiple energy blasts in hopes of hitting him, but each blast he fires does nothing.

Fraq appears behind Vyncent and slashes him to the back.

Vyncent yells out in pain. He turns around and aims his fist, but Fraq is no longer there. Fraq then appears behind Vyncent again and kicks him in the back to force him on the ground.

Upon landing, Vyncent flips around and punches the energy sword Fraq is thrusting at him.

Fraq swings the other sword, but Vyncent uses his forearm to deflect the blade and trips Fraq. Fraq forces his sword to disappear so he can use his hand to push himself back up. A war hammer is created instead of another sword.

Vyncent's eyes widen with surprise just before Fraq hits him across the face with the war hammer.

Immediately after, Fraq slashes Vyncent across his chest with the remaining sword. Fraq follows up by uppercutting Vyncent with the war hammer. The force from the blow knocks him into the air.

The sword morphs into a whip within a fraction of a second. Fraq cracks it against the ground and flings it towards Vyncent; it wraps around his ankle. Fraq pulls to bring Vyncent face-first onto the ground. The war hammer disperses so Fraq can grab his whip with both hands and slam Vyncent three more times. The whip disperses as a pair of flails with spiked mace balls form in his hands.

He approaches Vyncent and hits him on his back continuously with them. Even with his aura taking most of the damage, Vyncent still screams loudly from the pain.

After the first few blows, blood begins to come out of his mouth. With each strike, Fraq's smile gets bigger, and his eyes become deranged with enjoyment.

Fraq stops his onslaught and stands over Vyncent with much satisfaction. He opens his hands to make the flails disperse.

Wild energy begins to build. A massive war hammer forms that Fraq must wield with both hands. The length of it is thirty-five inches and the head of the hammer is twenty inches in width and length. He raises it overhead with a sadistic grin on his face.

Before he gets the chance to swing it, two small balls roll in front of him. The balls stop at his feet and begin to beep. Fraq looks at them with a confused expression. The balls beep more rapidly before exploding and creating a blinding light. Fraq disperses the hammer so he can shield his eyes.

A few moments pass before Fraq can see clearly. He realizes that Vyncent is nowhere to be found.

Chapter Five:

What Just Happened?

Desmond arrives in the lobby of SAGA Headquarters. As he makes his way through, every agent he passes gives him a warm greeting. The older agents simply offer him a salute.

He makes his way into the elevator and takes it all the way up to the floor where Kelly's office is located. He is walking down the hall with a grin on his face and an optimistic attitude. He reaches for the door, but his hand goes right through it. He examines his hand with a confused expression.

"What the hell?"

His hand has become transparent. Slowly, the rest of his body becomes incorporated as well until he completely withers away.

The door to Kelly's office opens. Kelly pokes her head into the hallway before she looks back at Karina.

"I promise you, I heard Desmond's voice."

Karina gives her a not so confident expression.

"Whatever, Kelly, you're just trying to get out of this conversation. Stop stalling and tell me where you stashed her. And I don't want to hear any of that top secret crap!"

Kelly rolls her eyes as she makes her way back into the room, the door slamming behind her.

Sometime later, Desmond finds himself awakening on the floor of what appears to be an enclosed cave. The dirt floor is bare, and he is surrounded by rock walls that don't seem to have an entrance or an exit.

Desmond stands up and admires the writing he sees on them. All over, there are many different passages mixed with various languages. They all run into each other in a way that makes it hard to understand what it means.

He turns around and looks to the center of the room. There is a constant yet gentle flow of bright, warm energy moving upward and downward in a spiral motion. He reaches out to touch it, but an energy field manifests and gives him a jolt. He jerks his hand back and the energy field becomes invisible again. He shakes his hand to help relieve the pain. He decides to look around some more until he suddenly hears a familiar voice.

"Hello, Desmond, it's nice to see you again."

He looks up and narrows his eyes.

"Who are you, and what am I doing here?"

The voice speaking to him does a humorous chuckle.

"I expected your first question to be, 'How did I get here.' Knowing you, you probably figured it out by now."

Desmond squints his eyes and snaps them back open when he realizes whose voice that is.

"Is that you, Berengia?"

In front of Desmond, energy begins to form into the shape of a person. Seconds later, Berengia's appearance manifests, but he is completely made up of energy the same way he had been in Desmond's subconscious.

Desmond takes a few steps to him.

"Next time you decide to summon me, a little warning would be nice. What is this place anyway?"

Berengia extends his arm.

"I call this place the Indigenous Bridge. It is a medium that exists between realms to serve as a haven. This will be a place of training and council for you in the times ahead."

Desmond looks at the flow of energy and then back at Berengia.

"And that?"

Berengia's expression hardens slightly.

"That is a containment unit created by me and my father. It houses the countless demon souls we trapped a few centuries ago during the Great Demon War. Even with our success, it's apparent Czar found a separate rift we created for the lesser demons. It was important to keep certain ranks separated."

"There's more to that story, but I feel like that's all I'm getting for now."

Berengia nods as he says, "For now."

Desmond nods his head in acceptance.

"Why did you wait until now to bring me here?"

Berengia begins to walk around him.

"It's been a long time since I've been here, and I needed to make it my own again. Timulus has kept me informed of the progress you have made, but I must be honest with you, it still isn't enough."

Desmond crosses his arms with an expression of agitation.

Berengia continues as if he didn't notice Desmond's annoyance.

"You have undoubtedly gained strength, but so has Czar. I discovered he has allowed his essence to be reborn through a human. I assume he thought this would gain him the ability to become limitless."

Desmond tightens his lips.

"If that isn't the way, then what is?"

Berengia looks at the flow of energy for a long moment.

"In order for you to progress further, you must become part demon."

Desmond unfolds his arms and looks at Berengia with fury in his eyes.

"Have you lost your damn mind?"

Berengia turns to face him while Desmond continues his rant.

"First you hijack my body, and naturally I inherit your fight against those aliens. Even after that, you give me the weight of the universe on my back. And now you want me to purposely become a demon? What more will you want from me? You want me to make you a spirit messiah baby, too? How about I give you my limbs while we're at it?"

Desmond turns around and stares at the flow of energy with much anger in his eyes.

Berengia sighs as he lifts his hand slightly. An image is created in front of Desmond. He looks at it to see the Earth in catastrophic panic.

The oceans have become drought, the lands have no vegetation, and severe weather plagues the whole planet.

Desmond gazes at it with a mix of fear and concern. He turns to face Berengia.

"What is this? Is that what the world will be reduced to if I don't do this?"

Berengia shakes his head.

"No. That's what the world would have been if I didn't choose you to begin with. I'm not omnipresent, but my abilities at rare moments will allow me to see where my opposite decisions would have led me. It only happens after I've made a crucial life choice.

When we first met, you recall I no longer had a physical body. I had no choice but to use my life-force to retain my spiritual form. I had no way to protect anyone. You, more than anyone, know that in desperate times, you must do what you can, what no one else will."

"Fine. I don't know if this is right, but I do know that evil escalates when we choose the easy route."

Desmond stands straighter as he makes a fist.

"I'll do it. I'm not going to grow a tail or horns, am I?"

"To be honest, the transformation can be random and unpredictable. I will do my best to extract a demon essence with the least disfiguration."

Timulus phases through a wall as he enters the room.

Berengia reaches his hand towards the containment unit.

"Timulus is here just as a precaution if anything goes wrong."

Desmond nods his head and braces himself.

The flow of energy begins to pulse as Berengia reaches his hand towards it. The energy is no longer calm, but now moving in a wild motion as if it senses danger. After seconds of concentration, a small strand is plucked away from it and taken out of the containment unit. The flow suddenly returns to a calm state.

Berengia guides the strand to Desmond.

"Just to be clear. This is what you want?"

Desmond closes his eyes and takes a deep breath.

"Let's get this over with."

The strand slowly enters Desmond's chest. A burgundy aura immediately surrounds his entire body. His muscles expand slightly as he feels the power coursing through him. His body lifts a few inches off the ground. He opens his eyes and brings his fist up to examine it.

"I have to admit, guys, this power feels overwhelming but amazing."

Desmond's body pulses which causes him to lose his breath for a moment.

Berengia looks at him with a concerned expression.

"Relax, Desmond. Feeling uncomfortable during the process is normal, but don't let it distract you."

"No," Desmond says. "It's not like that. It's something else, but I can't put words to it."

The burgundy aura surrounding Desmond has suddenly began to fade away. After the aura dissipates, an orange aura erupts from him and surrounds his body. Golden streaks of energy mix with his aura. Desmond's eyes widen as he grips his chest.

"Something's wrong!" Desmond shouts in a panic.

The aura has begun to wildly surge around his body. Timulus attempts to approach Desmond, but the aura shoots a bolt of energy on the ground in front of his feet.

"Master, you must stop this," Timulus says with concern in his voice.

"No," Desmond says with assertiveness. "I can take it!"

Berengia looks amazed and says, "Stand down, Timulus. We must see this through. Something is familiar about the power he is projecting."

Desmond's pupils disappear and his body relaxes as if the pain has subsided. His aura is still surging around him in an uncontrolled manner, but Desmond is showing no reaction.

Sparks begin to come from his aura. Then his body bursts into flames.

Timulus guards his face with his forearm. He shifts his eyes to Berengia and notices he has a fascinated expression on his face. Timulus forwards his attention back to Desmond who is not only showing an immense power but is also still engulfed in a raging flame.

Desmond looks straight up without showing any signs of pain. His skin begins to darken and reveal signs of third degree burning.

"Master, you must stop this! He could die!"

Berengia ignores Timulus' plea and continues to observe Desmond.

Desmond's body begins to pulse just as his pupils appear in his eyes. He looks around and looks himself over in a panic. He begins to scream, but nothing is coming from his mouth. His arms and legs stiffen as his head snaps upward. The flames engulf him completely to the point that Berengia and Timulus can no longer see him.

Berengia takes a few steps towards him and reaches both of his hands towards the flames. His eyes widen in surprise.

"I can't stop this."

Berengia slowly lowers his hands.

"What have I done?"

Desmond drops hard to the ground and the flames slowly begin to disperse. When the flames are completely gone, he is nothing but an unrecognizably burnt corpse.

Timulus and Berengia both look upon him disbelief and grief.

Berengia stares somberly into the distance as he says, "I'm sorry, Desmond. I honestly thought you were developing a power I once saw in a former ally. My arrogance has cost your life and that is unforgivable."

Timulus looks over at Berengia with a pained expression.

"I warned you to stop this! You should have performed this ritual on me first. As highly as you spoke of this human, I would have proudly given my life for his. He was our only hope to defeat Montezuma and his reign. What now?"

Berengia slowly turns to face Timulus.

"I am ashamed by what happened here, but it appears he's not our only hope. Maybe the taste of desperation was too great for me, and my judgment was flawed. Bring Vyncent to me."

Timulus looks at him with disgust, but he changes his attitude towards Berengia. He lowers his head with two tightly gripped fists.

"As you wish."

Mental Data Entry:

Zero-Nine

I'm aware that this entry is a slight jump from the fourth one, but you must understand my fury. The entries between this one and my last were nothing but a string of curses. Most of them were in languages I'm sure you've never heard of. I think I went temporarily insane with rage after what happened with Desmond.

Berengia's stupidity was the icing on the cake. He just stood there and let it all happen. Not only is that ritual unreliable, but it is dangerous because it has a very low survival rate. I'll give Berengia the benefit of the doubt, but I can tell you that he didn't know how fatal this risk was, but it doesn't mean I have to forgive him. His death threw a planet-sized wrench in my plans, and I don't know how to recover from it. I've allowed myself to think that maybe he isn't dead, but I can't feel his power at all. Right now, Berengia is at the source of my torment.

Chapter Six:
Battle of Wills

On the planet Pluto, there are multiple smaller villages on the outskirts of the main civilization. These villages are mostly made up of Plutonians who have similar life interest: Religion, mirrored personalities, physical activities, and even life partner matching. The villages are what keep the lives of the Plutonians vastly interesting and spontaneous.

Before Montezuma turned their way of life upside down, each village would meet in the main civilization for a big social gathering. The purpose of this was for each culture to bond with others.

There is one village that stands out significantly from the rest. The reason being is that this village educates on the teachings of the ancient history of why Pluto adopted the old ways of man from Earth. Even though it is an adopted way of life, they have reformed it to negate past mistakes of humans.

One village practices the traditions of monks by living their lives in prayer and study, but also by helping their fellow Plutonians when they are in need, no matter how small or extreme the task would be. This group of Plutonians are considered royalty amongst others because of the secrets they are entrusted with. They alone know the forbidden history of the ancient ways, and under no circumstances do they reveal them to anyone outside of their village.

Montezuma believes that part of the knowledge they guard is about the legend of Hurak.

Along with a handful of his followers, Montezuma arrives in the middle of the village with the elder Plutonian. He shoves him to the ground as he looks around.

"Elder, are you sure the answers to my questions are here? This village looks deserted. It's almost as if they were expecting me."

The elder looks at him with fear.

"I promise on the oath of the Blazed Bird. This is where they are."

Montezuma lifts the elder in the air by his neck and looks around.

"From what I hear, you all live with a purpose to help your fellow Plutonian!" Montezuma shouts to the empty-looking village. "If someone doesn't reveal themselves, I will snap his neck and burn this village to ashes!"

Moments after his announcement, a dozen of Plutonian monks slowly come out of their huts and approach him with their hands up. Every one of them seem to be of seasoned age. They are dressed in robes without any footwear. Once they are at a safe distance, they stop walking but one of them takes a few more steps. The apparent leader has a scar over his left eye and an old burn wound on the right side of his neck.

"I am Blez, the Abbot of this village and of this tribe. We know who you are and what you're seeking."

"Good," Montezuma says as he tosses the Elder onto the ground. "Then we don't have to waste time with threats and torture to get what I want."

All the monks lower their hands.

Montezuma smirks as he asks, "You're going to make me work for it, aren't you?"

"We are the last line of defense for the sons of this village! Know this, Montezuma, you will not get past us," Blez says.

Montezuma looks past Blez and asks, "They must be in that hut behind you?"

He crosses his arms and speaks with a commanding tone.

"Get them out of my way."

Before Montezuma's minions can make the first move, all the monks remove their robes and take a stance. Smoke rises from their physical bodies and their eyes begin to glow a faint gold glow.

Blez stomps his foot onto the ground.

"We have been blessed with the strength of the Blazed Bird. You will fall on this day, Montezuma!"

Montezuma minions stand ready while projecting their own auras.

Montezuma now looks annoyed as he thinks, *So, Berengia must have given them access to a rawer source of Spirit Energy. This should be interesting.*

The monks charge at the minions and begin hand to hand combat. One of the monks closes in on one of the minions and sucker punches him in the face. The minion regains his composure and strikes back, but the monk catches his fist to pull him closer and headbutt him. The monk knees him in the stomach and elbows him on the back of his neck causing him to drop to the ground.

Another minion launches at him from behind, but the monk leans sideways to evade the attack. Without hesitation, the monk grabs the second minion by the ankle in midair and slings him into another direction. He was thrown hard enough to make his body skip along the ground.

The first minion jumps up and punches the monk three times in the face. He goes in for a fourth, but the monk slaps his punch away and counters with an open palm. His hand stops just an inch from the minion's chest, but the force of his strike shatters the minion's rib cage as well as sending him flying a few yards away. He died instantly before hitting the ground.

The same monk joins his brother in another fight. They punch a brute minion at the same time, but this minion can hold his own far better than the rest. The minion blocks both of their fists with his forearm. The monks appear to be shocked by his strength and attack him head-on with a coordinated strike. The minion calmly blocks all their attacks, but he suddenly punches at their fist to create a stalemate. The monk's eyes widen just before this minion strengthens his aura and launches an energy wave from each fist that completely disintegrates their heads. Two monks close in and grab the brute minion by each arm to hold him in place. The brute attempts to break their hold but is unsuccessful.

Straight ahead, Blez is charging straight at him with a faint aura surrounding his right fist. The brute brings up his right leg and kicks the monk to his left, then uses his free hand to punch the other monk away from him.

At the last second, the brute catches Blez's forearm with both hands, but Blez punches him in the stomach with his left fist. Blez grabs the brute by the throat and slams him on the ground.

The brute punches Blez in the chest to get him away from him. He stands up and they begin a stare off.

After a few seconds, they charge at each other with strong auras around their bodies. They both throw a punch that connects and creates a shockwave. Without hesitation, Blez punches the brute across the face. In retaliation, the brute punches him back and they continuously exchange blows to the face. Suddenly, the brute punches Blez hard enough to cause him to stagger down to one knee.

The brute smiles and goes in for another attack, but Blez catches his fist just as his eyes glow brighter. The brute looks surprised until Blez hits him on the chest with a fist charged with Spirit Energy. The blow caves his chest in, and a hole is blown through it and out his back. He lowers his head with exhaustion as the brute's body falls to the ground.

With Blez's guard down, a minion appears and kicks him in the stomach. He attempts another kick, but Blez spins out of the way and jumps-kick the minion across his face, instantly breaking his neck.

Blez drops to both knees while breathing through exhaustion. He looks around and sees his fellow brethren still fighting. He looks to his left and notices Montezuma walking towards him.

In his path, a minion was thrown onto the ground. A monk jumps on top of him, but before he can punch him, Montezuma grabs his wrist and breaks his arm. While still walking, he grabs a passing monk by his throat and rips it out.

Blez looks horrified by Montezuma's strength and slowly stands with both fists ready. He catches his breath while he waits for the attack.

To the right of Blez, one of the monks is defending himself against two other minions. The minions are attacking him relentlessly, but the monk is deflecting their blows. The monk uses an opening and slaps a punch from one of the minions. The slap redirects his attack to the other. This makes them unbalanced and confused.

The monk forms a sign with his hands and fires a sharp energy blast that pierces both of their skulls.

A minion sneaks up and grabs the monk from behind. He struggles to break from the hold, but he can't seem to get free.

Another minion races in and fires an energy shot that goes through the both of them. His attack instantly kills them and flings their bodies to the ground. The minion turns around to find his next target, but an energy beam was fired that went straight through his chest. He looks down and sees blood gushing from him as he falls to the ground and dies. The monk he thought he killed used his last breath to make sure he didn't die in vain.

Blez witnessed that entire ordeal and he feels nothing but sadness. He stands tall and takes a step.

"Enough of this meaningless bloodshed!"

Everyone stops fighting and focuses on him.

"Let's finish this between us, Montezuma. We have both lost enough soldiers."

Montezuma smirks.

"The only difference is I have more to spare than you, but I accept your terms."

Blez stands ready as he says, "As you already figured out, the sons are in that hut. Defeat me, and only then may you pass. But as I said before, you will not get to them!"

Montezuma slowly vanishes, but reappears directly in front of Blez to punch him in the face. Without any hesitation, Blez catches his fist which impresses Montezuma. He head butts Blez and wraps his tail around his waist to slam him onto the ground. After his tail unravels, Montezuma jumps up and attempts to stomp his foot onto him, but Blez rolls out of the way and fires an energy shot with two fingers. Montezuma uses his tail to deflect it into another direction. The deflected energy shot ends up tearing one of his minions in half.

Montezuma forms an energy ball in his hand as he rushes at Blez and hits him in the stomach. Montezuma grabs Blez by the mouth and unleashes an energy blast. This attack knocks Blez on his back. Smoke is rising from his face. He screams from the pain as he struggles to get up.

Montezuma sneers at him.

"Is this the extent of your abilities? I've hardly even warmed up, insect."

Blez becomes angry as he stands with determination. A golden aura begins to surge around him like steam. His muscles expand and his resolve is now clearly showing. His eyes glow brighter just as the force of his rising power cracks the ground beneath him.

Montezuma looks surprised.

Blez's body becomes transparent, but then a solid version of himself appears in front of Montezuma that punches him in the face.

Montezuma feels the blood coming from his mouth. He strikes back, but Blez spins to the side to evade and uppercuts him.

Blez flip-kicks him and grabs tightly onto Montezuma's arm as he throws him a few yards away. Blez runs towards him and jumps into the air.

Upon descending, he spins with his arms out and fires a continuous beam of energy. Each blast hits Montezuma dead on. Once he gets closer to the ground, he stops the energy attack and strikes Montezuma over the head with both fists.

Montezuma grunts in anger and punches Blez in the stomach. He fires an energy blast that sends Blez flying.

Blez doesn't let that slow him down. He charges back at Montezuma and punches him in the face.

Montezuma elbows Blez in the stomach and follows with an uppercut.

In retaliation, Blez grabs Montezuma's arm and pulls him close to knee him in the stomach, but Montezuma catches his knee and throws him to create some distance.

They both stare each other down while breathing hard.

Within a fraction of a second, they rush each other, and their blows create a shockwave that makes everyone in the area fall to the ground. They are now locked in a stalemate making it unclear who struck who.

After moments pass, Blez coughs up blood as every bit of his aura disperses and he falls face first to the ground. Montezuma won the fight, but Blez managed to leave him with a deep wound on the right side of his chest.

Montezuma surrounds his left hand with an intense amount of Spirit Energy and uses it to sear his wound to stop the bleeding. He grunts from the pain but smiles from his victory.

While breathing with exhaustion, he begins to make his way to the hut where the sons are. Before he gets too close, the entire hut explodes with enough force to make everyone around stagger. Montezuma wipes the blood from his mouth and runs towards the now destroyed hut. He forms an aura around his hands and claps hard enough to distinguish the flames. He throws around debris until he finds three Plutonian teenagers. Their bodies are now burnt corpses.

From across the field, Blez lifts his head and gives a weak chuckle.

"I told you… you will not get to them."

He grins at Montezuma before his head falls back on the ground. He dies with that grin on his face.

The Elder bursts into a hilarious laughter he could no longer hold in.

"This is the code of the monks here. They are the last line of defense. If you get past them, then the sons will be killed before they can be used for evil. Your efforts were for nothing, you monster."

Montezuma's anger swells from hearing the Elder's words, and his laughter is the icing on the cake. His aura bursts to life as he screams with rage.

Montezuma charges at the remaining monks. They attempt to defend themselves, but he easily overpowers them.

He grabs one monk by the arm and punches right through his chest. He approaches another monk from behind and rips his spine out.

He gets between two monks, shoves his hands in their mouths and snatches their jaws off. He rips the arm off one of them, infuses it with his Spirit Energy and launches it through the stomach of another monk.

The last three monks tremble in fear but are too shocked by his ruthlessness to move. He rushes to them, stabs one through the heart with his tail, rips the head off the second monk and uses his Spirit Energy to disintegrate the top half of the last monk's body.

He slowly walks to the Elder with anger in his eyes. The Elder closes his eyes and Montezuma uses his tail to swiftly cut off his head.

"Burn this village to the ground," Montezuma says coldly to the rest of his army.

Chapter Seven:
The Patient is Awake

Doctor Edward Williams is carefully examining blood samples. He looks very amazed at what he is observing. J-Nel walks in with a worried expression.

"Is he going to be ok?"

Doctor Williams turns around and looks at Vyncent, who is on a medical table covered in bruises and wounds. Doctor Williams rubs his chin as he chooses his words carefully.

"Yes, he has a healing factor that is helping to repair his organs. Once that is done, his exterior should begin to heal as well. Your friend has a very interesting physiology."

J-Nel crosses his arms and leans against a wall with a thoughtful expression.

"I'll admit he did well out there. He was outnumbered and outmatched, but he held his own. Thanks again for helping me with perfecting my inventions by the way."

He looks at the metal bands on his wrist with an intense stare.

"With everything going on, I need to be able to pull my own weight. Desmond will not fight this war alone."

Vyncent wakes up in a panic, gripping his chest. He sits up and looks around the room. He looks at J-Nel with a confused expression.

"Jason? Where am I? What happened to the aliens I was fighting?"

J-Nel takes a few steps towards him.

"I distracted them long enough to get you out of there. You did good out there."

Vyncent rubs his stomach.

"It doesn't feel like it. Fraq nearly killed me."

J-Nel raises an eyebrow.

"Fraq? That's an interesting name. I observed your fight before I stepped in. Next time you face him, try to damage the armor on his back. I think that is what helps him construct his energy into weapons."

Doctor Williams walks up to Vyncent to check his pulse and uses a machine to scan him. He focuses on the reading for a moment before speaking.

"Yes, I viewed the footage from the bodycam J-Nel set up before he came to your aid, and I must agree with him. He is a formidable fighter, but he won't be much without the help of that device. Your vitals are stabilizing, but you will be sore for a few hours. You took a massive beating."

Vyncent stands and grunts as he holds onto his stomach. A worried look forms on his face as if he just realized something.

"There was a girl the aliens took hostage. Is she okay?"

J-Nel nods his head.

"She's fine and is receiving medical attention as we speak."

Vyncent sighs with relief.

A flash occurs as Timulus appears in front of them. Doctor Williams yelps from the surprise and drops everything he was holding. His hands are trembling hard as he places a hand on his chest.

"Holy child of Christ! What is with you people?"

Doctor Williams places his hand on the wall to guide himself out of the room.

"I swear you all will send me to an early grave."

Dr. Williams gently closes the door and sits in a chair nearby.

"Hey Timulus, long time no see. How's Desmond doing?" J-Nel asks.

Timulus looks at him with an unreadable expression.

"He has shown great bravery in his quest to become stronger," Timulus says.

J-Nel eyes him with suspicion.

"That's a little cryptic. Even for you."

Timulus ignores his comment and addresses Vyncent.

"Master Berengia would like to speak with you. He may have a way to make you stronger."

Vyncent's eyes widen with excitement.

"Really? This is great! You missed it, but I just had my ass handed to me earlier. When can we leave?"

Timulus places his hand on his shoulder, but Vyncent's catches J-Nel's glare. Timulus looks away as a flash occurs and they are both gone.

Doctor Williams walks back into the room. He can feel the tension radiating off of J-Nel.

"Are you okay?"

J-Nel doesn't answer. He simply leaves the room without saying anything.

Chapter Eight:
The Audacity

Timulus and Vyncent arrive at the Indigenous Bridge. Berengia is already there waiting for the pair. Vyncent looks around in awe until his eyes set on the smoldering corpse. He stares at it for a long moment before he looks at the two.

"I'd hate to see the other guy."

Berengia and Timulus glance at each other.

"Vyncent," Berengia says cautiously. "We have a situation and with much shame I must admit to an error on my part."

Vyncent now looks worried as his eyes return to the corpse.

Berengia continues.

"I attempted to elevate Desmond, but something went terribly wrong. I'm not sure what exactly happened during the process."

Before Berengia can continue his ridiculous explanation, Vyncent cuts him off with a serious expression.

"Are you trying to tell me you killed Desmond? That's his body over there?"

Timulus takes a few steps towards Vyncent to help explain.

"Accidentally, yes. I am truly sorry, but as you know, we have a greater threat to work together on."

Vyncent turns sharply to Berengia.

"So let me get this straight. You weren't man enough to sit us all down and admit what you've done? Instead, you want to distract yourself from your failing by trying to make me your next in line. You want to do to me what you've done to him, but this time, you can guarantee the same mistake won't happen?"

Berengia clears his throat.

"The latter is true. I can make you stronger without repeating the same mistake."

"No thanks! At this point, I can't trust you and I damn sure won't risk dying because of your antics. I'll become stronger, but on my own. And you."

Vyncent looks at Timulus and continues speaking with a disgusted tone.

"You had the audacity to try and lie to his own brother. I expected more honor from you. Take me back. Now."

Timulus places his hand on Vyncent's shoulder. A flash occurs and they both disappear.

Berengia is left alone with his shame. Vyncent's words replay over and over in his mind. He shakes his head to try and clear his thoughts.

He's right. I should have told them of my failure. I didn't have these doubts or setbacks on Pluto. I'm not used to using 'people' skills, but I must think of something. This will divide us, but at this point, it's no one's fault but mine.

Berengia slowly disappears.

Chapter Nine:
New Recruits

Fraq is kneeling before Czar with his head bowed. He has just finished explaining to Czar about their failure in the Forest Area of Seredia Island. After much uncomfortable silence, Czar stands up and looks down at Fraq who refuses to meet his gaze.

"Just so I understand," Czar says questionably, "you had him at your mercy? You practically beat him to the last inch of his life, and it was a human device that bested you in the end?"

Czar takes a few steps towards Fraq who has nothing to say. Czar takes a deep breath.

"Well, at least I know that the weak link has improved. It is of no consequence that you all failed. Honestly, I was hoping Desmond would be drawn out so I can hear of his progress."

Fraq looks up at him.

"That's right," Czar says. "I didn't expect you all to succeed. I expected to hear a report of your deaths."

Fraq lowers his head to hide the anger in his eyes. He relaxes his composure so his tone doesn't come off as disrespectful.

"Is there anything else we can do to make up for our failure?"

"Yes. I looked over your footage and I must applaud your use of your Soul Pack. Your comrades, however, did not show anything worth my mercy. I've killed the two useless pawns you were with."

Fraq's lips tightened from hearing those words.

"I know they were your brothers, but they don't have what it takes to serve me or my father's rule. I imported two soldiers my father was willing to spare. They share your unique fighting style when equipped with the Soul Packs."

From behind Fraq, two female Plutonians donning the same Plutonian armor approach and kneel next to Fraq.

The female to his left has an angularly spiked bang hairstyle. Majority of her hair is light brown with red and yellow tinting. She has a slender build and goes by the name Skuzy.

The other female has a more masculine build with a medium length ombre mohawk. Her mohawk is a bright sky blue with fading platinum highlights and closely cropped sides with a subtle blonde hue. Her name is Rei.

Czar turns his back to them.

"You may leave."

Without hesitation, all three of them rise and leave the room.

Shortly after, a short male Plutonian enters the room from a side entrance. He is skinny and sporting an intense teddy boy haircut with lavender coloring and hot pink tips.

This Plutonian is a scientist. Instead of donning armor, he wears a red laboratory coat with black fire designs on the shoulders and upper back. His name is Dib. He kneels to Czar with reverence.

"A transmission is coming in from Lord Montezuma."

Without giving Czar time to react, Dib reaches out his hand as a device on his wrist glows and projects a hologram of Montezuma.

Czar kneels.

"Hello, Father. Thank you for supplying me with more resources."

"I need to ask you something, and I need you to think very hard about your answer," Montezuma says.

Czar looks at the hologram to give his father his full attention.

"During your time with Berengia, has he ever mentioned a connection with the legend of Hurak and his Spirit Energy?"

Czar hesitates.

"No, Father. He has never mentioned the legend with me. The only secret he shared was how to activate the energy within other lifeforms."

Montezuma's aura darkens as he grows agitated.

"Fine. I didn't expect you to know anything. Keep doing your job unless you hear otherwise from me."

"Have you found a new lead?" Czar asks out of curiosity.

Montezuma narrows his eyes and says, "Maybe, but I'll be in touch."

The transmission ends just as Dib lowers his hand. Czar rises to his feet and thinks.

Now, that is interesting. Berengia once mentioned Hurak and the many special talents of the Blazed Bird, but I never considered a connection between them and Spirit Energy. If I could find out that secret before my father, I could crush him and rule in his place. I never intended to be his slave. Helping him was a necessary risk since I couldn't be at two places at once.

He looks at his scientist.

"Dib, keep me informed if you hear of any new discoveries."

Dib stands up as he bows his head.

"Yes, my liege."

In another room of the high-tech base, Fraq stares at the two new recruits. As he looks them over, he can't imagine that they are just as strong as he is. His Soul Pack powers up.

"I need to know if I can count on you. Come at me without holding back. Both of you."

The female Plutonians look at one another and then back at him.

"Are you sure? From what Dib tells me from his analysis, we are all well matched. The two of us could possibly overwhelm you," Skuzy says.

Fraq closes his eyes and doesn't say anything.

After the short silence, Fraq's aura forms and he launches himself at the females. He uses his Soul Pack to create a pair of dual khopesh swords.

He attacks Rei first, but she creates a halberd with her aura. Even with little time to react, she blocks his attack with the blade of her weapon. He maintains the stalemate to bring around his left sword, but an energy arrow strikes his hand, causing his sword to disperse. He looks to his left and sees Skuzy armed with an energy bow, another arrow at the ready. He raises an eyebrow to the skill she is showcasing.

Rei pushes him back and strikes at him, but he deflects the attack and creates another Khopesh sword in his left hand. He attacks her savagely while trying his best to make her construct disperse. Rei remains calm and holds her ground.

A second before his next strike, she disperses her halberd, ducks to the ground, creates a pair of eskrima sticks, and uses them both to strike him in the stomach. He staggers for a moment, but that second cost him greatly. Rei sweeps his legs out and causes him to fall on his back, then brings both sticks down on him. His swords disperse, but he forms a large shield to block her attack.

He pushes her off and knocks her across the head with it. He jump-kicks her, throwing her a few feet away from him. He slings his shield at her. Before the shield makes contact, a throwing axe stops it in midair as both weapons disperse.

Fraq creates a pair of dual butterfly swords and runs at Skuzy.

She concentrates and creates a spear in each hand. She narrows her eyes and throws them both.

Fraq dodges one and uses a sword to deflect the other.

Skuzy doesn't give up. She creates two more spears and launches them at Fraq. She continuously creates more and keeps throwing them as he gets closer.

Fraq expertly dodges and deflects the incoming targets until one of them manages to pierce his right shoulder.

After the successful strike, Skuzy takes a different approach and throws twenty shuriken at him. As the spear he was struck by disperses, he creates a pole arm to twirl as fast as he can to block all but six of the incoming shuriken. He staggers backwards as Rei approaches with a battle axe and slashes him on his back.

Without hesitation, she turns her axe and hits him over the head with the blunt side of her axe.

Fraq falls to the ground.

Before Rei can attack him again, he holds up a palm as a gesture of surrender. Satisfied by this, the females disperse their weapons and help him to his feet.

"Ok, you two have made a believer out of me," Fraq says.

Rei snorts with indignation.

"I tried to warn you."

He looks to Skuzy with a questioning expression.

"You two are quite impressive. I thought I was the only one who could throw constructs, but you have more of a handle on them than I ever have."

Rei shrugs.

"Ranged attacks are more Skuzy's specialty, especially when it comes to precision. Berengia trained us to be a team and a force to be reckoned with on the battlefield. Our techniques could change the tide of any battle. Czar didn't know about us at first because we were a unit Berengia kept separately."

Fraq stands up straight and eyes them both wearily.

"How do I know you won't turn on me later for Berengia and his human?"

Rei looks at him with a blank expression.

"We follow who shows their dominate strength. Right now, that would be Montezuma. Berengia lost to him, so that makes him our new leader."

Fraq looks them over again but decides he is satisfied with their answer.

"I'm going to the medical bay to get cleaned up. Find me when we have orders."

Fraq leaves the room.

Rei and Skuzy exchange a look of intensity.

Chapter Ten:
The Truth is Out

At SAGA Headquarters, Vyncent has just finished telling everyone about what happened to Desmond and how Berengia tried to avoid talking about his death. Timulus decided to stick around for the conversation on account of his own guilt. He wanted to be there to answer any questions, but to also take any blame anyone wanted to point.

After the explanation, no one says a word.

J-Nel gets up to his feet and approaches Timulus. They stare at each other for a long moment until J-Nel breaks the silence.

"I appreciate you for staying while Vyncent told on your boss. I don't blame you for lying to me. You're just a soldier following orders. With that in mind, whatever happens next, I expect you to be on the front lines whenever Czar makes his move. Regardless of what

Berengia says, you owe that responsibility to Desmond. You want to make amends? Do it by fighting in my brother's place."

Before Timulus can respond, J-Nel leaves the room. Timulus looks at everyone else with an apologetic expression.

"I will do as he says. He is right, and not only to Desmond, but I also owe it to all of you to fight by your side."

With a flash, Timulus disappears.

The room was quiet until Karina burst into tears and spoke with raw pain.

"I refuse to believe he's gone. Not like that. His death was not meant to come by some damn experiment!"

Kelly doesn't make a move to comfort her or to give her words of encouragement. Instead, she folds her hands onto her desk and just stares off into space.

"If you need me, I'm going to train," Vyncent says.

Kelly simply nods her head while Karina continues to cry.

Vyncent leaves and heads straight to the training room with fierce determination in his eyes.

Outside of SAGA Headquarters, J-Nel is walking towards a motorcycle until he suddenly smells something burning. He turns around and his eyes widen.

In the air across from him is a small ball of fire. It twists and forms into a foreign phrase.

"سوف يعود."

J-Nel quickly takes out his phone and snaps a picture. Just as the picture is taken, the fire dies down and withers away without leaving any evidence of its existence behind. J-Nel checks the image to search for its meaning. He looks thoughtfully and thinks.

This is Arabic?

He types a few commands on his phone to translate.

Before his phone can show him the results, his phone alerts him to an incoming call from Doctor Williams.

With a raised eyebrow, he accepts the call. Immediately, he hears voices on the other end.

"I know the human is around here somewhere. We traced that low tech garbage right here," a voice says.

J-Nel puts the phone on speaker as he listens intently.

A different voice then says, "Don't stress, Valp, he's only one human, and there's nothing threatening about him. Czar just wants us to bring back his head for proof that we got the job done. Serves the human right for thinking he could outsmart us."

Without waiting to hear more, J-Nel mutes his end of the call and rushes back inside SAGA.

Chapter Eleven:
Panic Before Reason

At the Observatory, Doctor Williams is cowering under his desk while Plutonian soldiers are tearing his lab apart.

The cloaking device Doctor Williams is using allows him to hide in plain sight. It's a solid plan really, except for the fact that the device only holds enough power for forty-five minutes, and he spent thirty minutes in the fetal position under his desk before thinking about calling J-Nel. He was relieved after listening to J-Nel taking action with the others.

Glancing at the clock on the wall, he sees that he will only be invisible for the next seven minutes.

Doctor Williams considers himself a disciplined man. During this entire time, not once did he make any unnecessary noises or move even a single inch.

As he thinks that he may die here, he lets out a deep, loud sigh.

Just like that, the entire room becomes so quiet, you could hear a leaf fall outside.

He stiffens just as he realizes the mistake he made.

Valp pauses his movements with a chair in his hands.

Valp's golden hair covers half of his face and reaches down past his shoulders on one side of his head; the other side is shaven. He squints his eyes as he looks around the room.

"Did you hear that? I think our human has finally lost his nerve," Valp says with satisfaction.

The air in the room becomes deathly still. The other soldier, Gol, walks towards the desk and gazes at it with a confused expression.

Gol has a shaved head with a thick braid down the back. His braid consists of strands of purple, navy blue, and silver.

Still invisible, Doctor Williams looks up at the Plutonian and mentally recites a prayer.

Suddenly, the lights go out. Gol stands up straight with a worried expression.

"What's going on? Did you do this, Valp?"

"No," Valp exclaims. "Maybe we messed up the wiring in this place when we first got here."

A different voice is heard within the darkness of the room.

"Coming here was a mistake you won't live to regret."

Before the two soldiers could respond, a quick bolt of light shot out and made impact on Gol's face, sending him flying backward.

Valp yelps in surprise while powering up his Soul Pack to produce a mid-sized energy rifle. His weapon gives off enough light so he can see his surroundings.

He looks to his left and sees that Gol has a gaping hole where his face used to be.

He swallows hard and randomly fires his rifle around the room in a wide sweep. He stops firing and listens carefully. He turns around and his light illuminates J-Nel's angry face. Valp flinches in surprise, but because of his hesitation, J-Nel was able to punch Valp directly in his throat causing him to disperse his construct of the rifle.

The room becomes pitch black again. Doctor Williams feels a glimmer of hope until he hears bones break under someone else's assault. He wonders if those terrible sounds are coming from J-Nel's body. He hears another breaking of bones until he hears Valp's voice.

"Please stop! I was only following orders!"

Before Valp can plead more, Doctor Williams hears a gurgling sound until silence surrounds him again.

The lights in the room come back on to reveal J-Nel and Karina standing in front of him. That's when he notices that his device ran out of power. He looks at the clock and back at his rescuers with amazement.

"You two are scary and amazing at the same time. That literally only took you guys one minute and twenty-three seconds.

Karina chuckles with amusement.

"They would have been dead sooner if J-Nel didn't insist on toying with the poor aliens."

J-Nel shrugs as he helps Doctor Williams to his feet. J-Nel looks around the destroyed lab before he refocuses back on Doctor Williams.

"I've told the others what we've been up to while we were on our way here. It's decided it's safer to move you to SAGA Headquarters for the time being. Do you have any idea why they went through the effort to try and kill you?"

"Yes," Doctor Williams says with confidence.

"I discovered what Czar is up to."

Chapter Twelve:
Who is She?

Karina and J-Nel stare at Doctor Williams as if he just sprouted horns from his head. For the first in a long time, J-Nel is so shocked that his jaw is slightly dropped. Seeing this expression on his face brings satisfaction to Doctor Williams.

Around them, there are SAGA operatives packing up any necessary equipment.

Karina is the first to regain her composure.

"We're going to need to tell everyone else what you just told us. This is crazy."

J-Nel shakes his head in an attempt to wipe away his astonishment.

"And you have proof?"

Doctor Williams walks over to a wall behind his desk and places his hand on a specific spot. A panel glows and opens to reveal a hard drive plugged into the interior. Doctor Williams carefully removes it and holds it up for them to see.

"Any information I discovered is backed up to a secure server, but in case that server is compromised, my backups are safely stored on this. I have concrete evidence on what Czar has done and is still doing."

Karina looks up towards the massive hole in the ceiling to see an approaching helicopter with Vyncent trailing next to it. The helicopter and Vyncent both land in front of the Observatory. Karina meets them outside.

"Thanks for escorting the helicopter, Vyncent. We wanted them covered in case they were discovered."

Vyncent shrugs and looks at the battered building.

"I'm all about teamwork, Karina."

Doctor Williams gives the SAGA operatives a final list of what he needs brought to headquarters before allowing J-Nel to guide him to the helicopter. Doctor Williams and Karina climb inside.

Vyncent looks at J-Nel.

"You're not going with them?"

J-Nel closes the door to the helicopter and faces Vyncent.

"We need to talk. Walk with me."

As the helicopter takes off, they begin their walk through the forest.

After walking in silence for thirty minutes, Vyncent clears his throat.

"I thought you wanted to talk," Vyncent says cautiously.

J-Nel glances at him for a moment before forwarding his attention straight ahead again.

"Inside the Observatory, I was able to beat down one of those aliens. I even managed to break some of its bones before killing it."

Vyncent raises an eyebrow to that. Vyncent clearly remembers the amount of force he had to dish out when fighting Fraq and his henchmen. Their armor were tough nuts to crack. He struggled with his Spirit Energy, but J-Nel took down one of them with ease. Vyncent is now more intrigued as to how J-Nel accomplished that.

"My point of revealing this to you is to show that the tides are shifting around us, Vyncent. We must trust each other because there are forces out there that don't have our best interest in mind."

"When you say forces, you must mean Berengia?" Vyncent asks.

J-Nel slows his pace for a fraction of a second, then continues the pace he began with.

"Yes," J-Nel says in a bitter tone.

He lifts his arm to show Vyncent a titanium band on his wrist.

"I didn't take you for an accessory guy," Vyncent says jokingly.

J-Nel explains further as if he didn't hear him.

"I have one of these on each wrist. There is a field covering the skin on my body that's invisible to the naked eye. It allows me to absorb kinetic energy and send it back with a concentrated strike. Like with a punch or kick to my enemies. I can absorb quite a lot and can dish it out when I choose."

Vyncent stops walking and stares at him with an open mouth.

"Jason, that's amazing."

J-Nel stops walking to face him and continues to explain.

"Too much absorption can put a strain on my body and heart. My point is that, if faced with a decision to take on more kinetic energy than I can handle, I will take it if it means saving the world and ending the mission Desmond started."

Vyncent and J-Nel stare at each other until Vyncent nods his head.

"I understand. I trust you. Trust me to also do the same if necessary."

J-Nel gives him a slight grin as he turns to continue walking.

Vyncent follows and notices a log cabin ahead of them. He starts to tell J-Nel they should go another way, but a beautiful woman comes around the corner of the cabin with an axe in hand. She picks up a log off the ground and sets it on a tree stump. Without much effort, she chops the log in half. Vyncent stares at her as if starstruck until he realizes he's seen this woman before. His foot crunches a twig, making a snap that sounded louder than necessary.

Without any hesitation, the woman throws the axe in Vyncent's direction. He immediately freezes due to the surprise of the precision of her throw. The axe digs deep into the tree just mere centimeters from his head. He looks to his left and swallows hard as he stares at the blade of the axe.

J-Nel chuckles as he shakes his head with amusement.

"Sorry we startled you."

The woman doesn't look amused. She looks at them both and seems to have come to a decision. She rubs her left forearm and now has a playful expression on her face.

"Sorry about that. You won't believe the bold animals that live around here," she says with a soft African accent.

She gives them a big smile.

"It's a good thing I'm rusty at axe throwing."

Vyncent recovers and snatches the axe from the tree. He mentally notes that he had to put a little effort into taking it out. He looks to her.

"Hey, aren't you the woman I met at the bar the other day. Your dad died, right?"

Her smile slips slightly.

"Yeah, that sad and drunk girl was me. My name is Christina. I hate that you saw me in such a state."

She meets them halfway and takes the axe from Vyncent.

"What are you doing out here?" Vyncent asks.

She makes a show of stretching before she responds.

"Well, after my dad's funeral, I discovered that Seredia Island has cabins that people can rent out for extended time periods. This place was on his bucket list, so I figured I'd stay a while and see what the fuss is about. So far, I can see why he wanted to come this way. It's nice. What about you two?"

J-Nel looks her in the eye.

"We're just passing through. Wanted to show my friend here the 'untamed nature' and all her hoards."

A few beats pass as J-Nel and Christina stare at one another. Vyncent couldn't help but notice that it seemed like tension was radiating off Christina in thick waves. Christina takes a step back and puts a smile back on her face.

"I'll let you guys get back to it then. It's about to get dark soon and I need to get a fire started."

Without another word, she turns to grab her firewood and calmly walks into her cabin.

"What was that all about?" Vyncent asks.

J-Nel begins walking with Vyncent following behind him.

"Just another tourist I suppose," J-Nel says.

From the window and through the slit of her curtains, Christina watches them leave with an intense look in her eyes.

She thinks, *I have to watch out for that one.*

Chapter Thirteen: Good News at Last

Montezuma is levitating in the atmosphere of Pluto with his aura flaring. In a meditative state, he marvels for a moment just how far this planet has come. He remembers from long ago that his people were in a primitive age for their species. They barely had a lick of technology worth bragging about. Then that fateful day came and Berengia stumbled upon them. He and that elf-eared fool was so young then. They thought that together they could move Pluto into a position of power within the Spectrum.

Well, at least that's what Montezuma wanted.

Back then, he was the light that motivated his people. Sure, his ways of leadership could come off as a tyrant, but leading sometimes calls for a strong hand.

Before Berengia brainwashed his people to turn against him, Montezuma kept them fed, formed them into strong fighters, and even provided education in the art of war. All it took was some training camps to ensure their loyalty to him as their king. But no, Berengia put the idea in their heads that equality was better, and a leader should work for the people instead of the other way around.

Nonsense.

Back then, they may have managed to banish him, but now his time has come. He is sure of it.

Montezuma disperses his aura sensing that someone was about to approach him. He opens his eyes to see from a distance that one of his generals is flying towards him. He remembers giving the command that if he's disturbed while meditating, whoever disobeys the order will be punished by a painful death. He hadn't decided if it would be quick or slow yet. With this knowledge, he thinks that it must be worth it to risk his wrath.

The general stops about ten feet away from Montezuma. Montezuma thinks it's laughable that he thought by being out of arms reach he would be safe.

The general, known as Pican, bows with his head lowered. He stays in that position while he addresses Montezuma.

"I beg your forgiveness for this intrusion. By decree, this act of violating your privacy grants death, but by your words there are exceptions."

Montezuma looks Pican up and down before responding.

"This is very bold of you, general. Tread lightly and consider your next words carefully. Whatever you came to report better be worth your life."

A bead of sweat trickles down the back of Pican's neck.

"Yes, my liege. We have found the prison pods."

Pican stays silent to allow this information to sink in. Montezuma's eyes widen with surprise and excitement at the implications. No one knows who's in those pods except himself. Unlike his other projects, this is something he kept close to the chest. Many members of Pluto's civilization are newer generations and would not have been present during his fall from grace. Of course, there are a handful of elders who may have an idea. Montezuma collects himself.

"Where?"

Pican, still bowed, says, "They have just placed them in your throne room, but there is one complication. No one seems to know how to open them, and if we try to force them open, the subjects inside seem to suffer. It appears to operate as a failsafe. If tampered with, the pods will kill those inside."

Montezuma is annoyed by this news, but at the same time, he is elated. Without a word, Montezuma skyrockets towards the civilization.

Pican straightens himself and takes a deep breath.

"I need to get better at sensing the short straw to avoid being the messenger all the time. He's going to kill me one of these days."

In one of the camps stationed on the outskirts of the civilization, there is a Plutonian doctor treating patient wounds. He has the final say so whether a Plutonian can keep working or not.

His name is Kogi. His hairstyle is a simple bowl cut that is mostly orange with blue highlights that shimmer as he moves.

Kogi is like a medical machine. He can look at a patient and determine their ailments and treatment in less than five minutes. There are cases where research is necessary, but ninety-eight percent of the time, he can sort through patients rapidly. After making his final rounds of the day, Kogi steps outside to breathe in the chilly air.

He smiles up at the sky until he sees something strange. It looks like a red ball of death hurtling towards him, but, as it gets closer, it almost looks like a person.

Before he can speculate further, Montezuma flies towards him with amazing speed and lifts Kogi into the air without slowing down. Other Plutonians who were outside gaze after them while trying to wave off the dirt that got kicked up.

Nearby, there is a female Plutonian scientist standing on the roof of one of the Science Division buildings. Her name is Mila. She has long burgundy hair with eccentric curls down to her back. The tips of her hair have a sapphire blue tint to them.

This division's purpose is to monitor the vitality of the planet as well as work together to invent innovations that will benefit all Plutonian life. As of late, their research has been turned on its head. Ever since Berengia lost to Montezuma, the planet has suffered damage that threatens their natural resources. Nothing that would cause immediate alarm, but still, something to keep an eye on.

She is currently going through information in the Bio-Link implanted at the top of her spine. The Bio-Link connects all scientists to their servers so they can efficiently share or comb through information without needing to carry around any pesky tablets. Each scientist also controls what information they want stored privately or publicly with other scientists.

The Bio-Link has even made computers unnecessary in the division. Whenever a scientist is active with their Bio-Link, their eyes take on a green tint. Because of this feature, other scientists would know not to interrupt. Only members of the division have access to the implant and can only interact with the servers while in range of one of their buildings. The latter rule doesn't apply to higher ranking scientists, of course.

Mila disconnects from the server and looks over the terrain in front of her. She wonders how much worse the planet will get if Berengia isn't able to come back for them. She knows he's not dead, but she is aware of the state he was in when he fled. It's been a long time, but she keeps hope in her heart that change will come.

These days, her research has been focused on making upgraded Soul Packs and inventing devices to penetrate that door that was found recently. Rumors say saying that it is tied to the Hurak legend, but she has little faith in childish fables.

She sighs as she thinks of how her life is now. She looks to her left and spots an unfamiliar red glow on the horizon.

Is that a meteor? Mila thinks. *No, it can't be. Meteors don't behave like that, and they usually come from the sky.*

As it gets closer, she recognizes that it's someone flying across the terrain heading her direction. It also looks like whoever that is, is also flying with another person in tow. Before she can ponder further, Montezuma closes the gap and snatches her up.

Moments later, Montezuma rushes into his throne room and drops his captives onto the floor unceremoniously.

Mila and Kogi slowly rise to their feet and brush off the dirt and dust from their faces and clothes. They glance at each other before they forward their attention to Montezuma who has his back to them. He's staring at two large pods. They both kneel to him with their heads bowed. Montezuma turns to them.

"I have asked around and everyone agrees that you two are the most brilliant minds on the planet. Mila, you are not high ranking in the Science Division, but it has been proven your intellect and ideas vastly outpace the top ranks. From what I heard, you have refused to be promoted."

Mila stiffens.

"That is correct, my liege."

Montezuma now looks at Kogi.

"Then there's you, a doctor who was offered a seat in the Science Guild as one of The Four."

Mila snuck a look at Kogi. Mila refused her promotion because she hates the political side of being in the top ranks, but refusing to be a part of the Science Guild seemed blasphemous even to her. Having a seat with the Guild was a position of power any scientist would jump to. Not just for the power alone, but because of the monumental changes one could make to benefit Pluto. Membership in the Guild is a lifelong position, so they only invite someone when a current member dies. Even so, getting into the Guild is rare as there are only four seats available.

Kogi clears his throat.

"That is correct, my liege. I like the freedom of being immersed with the people I am helping. The Guild requires seclusion with their work and goals. Making waves without being seen is their primary philosophy. Admirable, but that is a lifestyle not suitable for me."

"You two are very interesting creatures, but I didn't bring you here to force you to take on those roles."

They both look up to him with a curious expression. He steps out of the way so they can see the two prison pods.

"I need your combined intellect to figure out a way to open these pods without endangering who is inside. My soldiers will be moving them to a lab nearby with everything you need. If you need anything that the lab doesn't have, just ask for it and it will be brought to you."

Montezuma begins walking out of the throne room.

"Perform this task as if your lives depend on it. Because they do. Get these prison pods open without killing the subjects inside."

After he has left, Mila and Kogi look at each other in shock and horror. At the same time, they are both wondering just how they got into this situation. They performed their skills in society under the radar for this exact reason. They guess it can't be helped when others notice your talents. They nod to each other and approach the pods.

"First of all, what in the Blazed Bird's name is a prison pod?" Mila asks.

Chapter Fourteen:
Deserved Guilt

Failure isn't something people tend to accept. It can fester and drive a person mad thinking of all the things they could have been done differently. The next stage with failure comes pride. Pride makes you incapable of fully admitting how wrong you were. After that comes self-loathing and a slew of other emotions that attempts to trick your mind into believing that your actions were justified. In an instant, all of this has hit Berengia like a wrecking ball.

Within the walls of the Indigenous Bridge, Berengia is in his energy form pacing back and forth. He has no need to do this since his essence is everywhere within this realm. Unfortunately, his guilt is making him do irrational things. He's even chastised himself for suggesting that Vyncent is the answer. Not that Vyncent can't be helpful. It's just that Berengia knows deep down that Vyncent doesn't have the innate potential Desmond had.

With a flash, Timulus appears before him with an unreadable expression. Berengia stops his pacing to look at him. They stare at each other for a while until Timulus breaks the silence.

"I've told the others what happened here. I placed my faith in you since my creation. Not once have I questioned you. Before today, I never considered for a second that your judgment was flawed. But after what I witnessed from your mistake with Desmond..."

Timulus drags a hand over his jaw as he works to compose himself.

Berengia looks down at his feet before locking eyes with Timulus again.

"What happened with Desmond was tragic, I know, but even you must admit the potent energy he was displaying. It reminded me of the power from the Idols."

Timulus clenches his fist so tightly he can feel the break of his skin. He looks at Berengia with disgust.

"The Idols? You toyed with his life because of a fable? I know you believe the Idols still exist, but this is a reach."

Berengia shakes his head.

"Timulus, listen."

Timulus flares his aura out like a shockwave that immediately causes Berengia to stop talking.

"No," Timulus says with resolve. "Berengia, you need to get a handle on this. You've lost the humans' trust as well as mine. I don't know what will become of us when it's time to face Czar, but I know I will do what I can with or without you."

Without waiting for a reply, Timulus leaves with a flash trailing after him.

Berengia stares for a long moment at the space Timulus was occupying. Inside, he knows that Timulus is right. He just doesn't know how to fix it. All he can think to do is…

"Wait."

Berengia jerks his head upward.

"I sense a familiar energy from long ago, but that's impossible."

He stands there with a childish grin on his face.

"Maybe there is a way for me to fix this."

His energy form disperses.

Chapter Fifteen:
He Did What!

There is something to be said about the life that surrounds us. What most people fear is the unknown that cannot be seen. The unknown that seems so impossible that it must be irrational and ignored. Only brilliant minds on the planet can accept there is more than just their own surroundings. One mind in particular is Doctor Williams. He came face-to-face with something so mind-blowing that he would accept being called crazy. What he didn't expect was a room full of people who not only believed him, but also looked to him for more answers.

Kelly, Vyncent, Karina, J-Nel and Timulus are all standing in the training room staring at Doctor Williams as if he has just presented the hardest mathematical equation to ever exist. Before them, Doctor Williams is standing with six, large eraser boards full of words and numbers.

J-Nel and Karina are standing stone faced. Kelly has taken a seat on the floor Indian style. Vyncent is unable to find a comfortable position, so he leans against a wall only to stand from it and then lean on it again. The only person in the room who isn't overwhelmed is Timulus. Kelly clears her throat to break the silence.

"Doctor Williams, You just threw a lot at us, and I must admit this all seems fantastical. What do you mean by another dimension?"

Doctor Williams briskly walks over to the third eraser board.

"There has always been talk in the scientific community about the theories of multiversal existence. Czar has proven that it not only exists, but it's also possible to create or stumble upon a dormant reality. What Czar is doing sets a tone that the universe is larger than anyone can imagine. The gateway I found is acting like a doorstep to another universe!"

Doctor Williams is so excited that he cannot control his giddiness. He turns and activates a holo-screen to show a clip of footage. The clip shows a point of view from a drone as it makes its way towards the gateway. While in the midst of passing through, the feed becomes distorted for almost a full minute until it clears again. Kelly stands up and eyes the feed with suspicion.

"The gateway leads to our headquarters?"

Doctor Williams shakes his head.

"Yes, but not yours."

Kelly looks at him quizzically and then back at the feed.

Doctor Williams continues to explain.

"I programmed the drone to hover around for five minutes and immediately come back the way it came in case it lost its connection to my manual controls. I had a hunch that would happen."

During the hover, the drone was able to capture a three-sixty view of the surrounding area.

"You see! It's an exact replica of the island."

A Plutonian soldier pops into view of the feed. He has the drone in his grasp and hurls it back into the gateway. After it makes its way to the other side, the feed is interrupted.

"After the drone was thrown back, its data was uploaded as soon as it connected to my server. That right there is proof that multiple universes exist."

"That's not what we saw," Timulus says in a serious tone.

Everyone gives him their full attention.

"What you all know as the universe is really called 'The Spectrum.' To be exact, its true name is now the 'Shattered Spectrum.' In a way it can be viewed as a multiverse, but a multiverse, to my understanding, is countless universes where different choices were made. So, if we live in a multiverse, that means, there's a world where J-Nel became Berengia's warrior instead of Desmond."

J-Nel's eye twitches at that notion.

"The Shattered Spectrum is not a multiverse. It is a collection of different dimensions that are separated, but at one point in time were one. When they were one, it was simply called The Spectrum because of all the different types of life. But one day a cosmical disaster took place and shattered everything into pieces. The dimensions are still somewhat connected, but they are also guarded by what you humans would call 'gatekeepers.' What Doctor Williams showed us was something entirely different then what exists in The Spectrum."

Doctor Williams brings back up the feed to the moment the drone is surveying the environment. Once there is a full view, he pauses it. Timulus steps closer and gestures towards the feed.

"What do you see?"

Everyone except for Doctor Williams gazes at the feed with confusion. Without waiting for a reply, he continues.

"Look closely at the streets and buildings. There are no people living their lives. There are no animals being curious of what's around them. There is nothing there but still air being occupied by no one except for Czar and his minions. That is not a dimension born from the Spectrum. That is a mirrored version of your world and your world alone. He played with the fabric of reality just so he could plan without interference. I'd even wager that he plans to fight you all in that mirrored dimension of his."

Everyone gapes at him as if he just told them the tooth fairy is real. No one speaks for a long moment until J-Nel speaks up.

"Alright. Mirrored dimension or not, we'll need to be prepared for whatever comes next. We have Timulus' support, my new tech, Vyncent has more control, and Karina has her own ace in the hole."

Karina glares at him, but he pretends not to notice. He continues.

"If Czar has all that time and space to prepare, then we must imagine the worst-case scenario."

Kelly looks at him unblinking as she says, "You think he's gathering enough forces for an invasion on a scale that's designed to overwhelm us."

J-Nel nods in confirmation of her statement.

"There's no telling how much time we have, but we need to pull miracles from anywhere we can. Timulus, would you be able to help Vyncent even further with his power?"

Timulus nods in acceptance.

"Kelly, can you help Doctor Williams improve Karina's symbiotic nanite armor?"

Kelly does a double take at him before she fixes Karina with a hard stare.

"What symbiotic nanite armor?"

Karina glares absolute death at Jason, but her scrutiny is humbled by the look of utter fury on Kelly's face. Doctor Williams on the other hand can't help but think of the fun he'll have with a nanite project.

"I'll let you two sort that out. In the meantime, I know we're all hurting from what happened to Desmond. He would want us to continue fighting. We'll finish the battle and mourn properly later."

Everyone appears to look solemn. After a pregnant silence, J-Nel's watch sends out an audible alert with a chime sound. He looks at his phone in response and grins slightly.

"I have to go. You all know your jobs. Hack away at whatever you need to do until Czar shows signs of surfacing."

Without another word, J-Nel storms out with determination carved into his expression.

Somewhere far away, but at the same time very close, a monitor is displaying the conversation the group just had. Down to the very detail without any delay of transmitting.

Czar stands in front of the monitor with a scowl on his face and a tightly clenched fist. His anger riles his aura to flare with so much energy it causes the ground beneath him to scorch. Just as quickly, he calms down and allows his aura to disperse as he turns around to his army.

He faces rows upon rows of Plutonian soldiers. Each soldier is equipped with upgraded Soul Packs that appear as slim versions of the originals. More lightweight, more powerful, and can even withstand a few hits from energy blast. At glance, it would appear there are at least a hundred soldiers in the room.

"No matter," Czar says with a cool demeanor. "With the human Desmond out of the way, I have no doubt we will succeed. Especially with our unknowing little spy. Thank you for your efforts, Fraq."

In the middle of the front row, Fraq kneels to Czar with pride in his posture. Czar looks back at the monitor that shows the point of view is coming from Vyncent.

"Yes," Czar says. "The Bio-Tap you injected him with is working flawlessly."

Chapter Sixteen:
The Lazuli

Later that night, someone breaks into an office in the Industrial sector. This person quietly slips in the door and begins to search around in the darkness. This person is skilled at making their way around without any hint of a light.

They shift through a file cabinet without making a mess. No need to leave evidence that anyone was here, after all.

Next are the drawers at the desk. Nothing turns up there, so the focus is now on the laptop. They open it to find a lock screen that requires a password which causes a grunt of frustration from the intruder.

Suddenly, metal shutters descend to cover every window and the door that they entered the office through. The person looks frantically around and sees there's no way out. What makes matters worse, it is completely dark, and they know just who to blame for this transgression.

The lights in the room flick on to reveal Christina at the desk and J-Nel leaning against the wall in a corner on the opposite side of the room. She looks at him with so much impatience that J-Nel finds it comical.

"Did you really think it would be that easy to just waltz within a mile of my domain without me noticing?" J-Nel asks mockingly.

Christina comes from around the desk to stand just a few feet away from him.

"Can you blame me? Especially after that comment at the cabin. I need to know what you know about me," Christina says with a hint of anger.

"Which part exactly?"

Christina loses her temper.

"Cut the shit! Does 'the untamed nature and all her hoards' ring any bells?! Lucky for me, your friend was too dense to realize you basically announced that I'm a dragon."

J-Nel, still relaxing against the wall, looks at her unblinkingly.

"Well, are you a dragon?"

Christina scoffs as she turns her back to him before facing him once more.

"Tell me what you think you know, and I'll fill in the blanks. As much as I can, anyway."

This omission intrigues J-Nel to the point he gets off the wall and looks at her intensely. He ponders on what to say as he strokes his goatee.

"I'll admit, I don't know much. Your people have made an impressive reputation at staying secretive, but even the best of secrets isn't immune to rumors. My suspicion is you're a blood relative to the Lazuli Spirit Clan that dates back so far that no one can pinpoint its origins. The most concrete rumors say that your clan's strength is connected to the spirit of a dragon that still exists in this world. What makes your clan so interesting is that it not only has its own unique martial arts style, but the clan also has in-depth knowledge of every martial art to ever exist. In doing so, it allows the clan to combine multiple arts into a variety of battle styles so deadly that countries are willing to pay top dollar for just a sliver of those techniques."

Christina remains silent.

"I believe the story about what happened to your father. What I don't believe is the reason why you're here. I'm willing to bet my entire business that you were sent here to investigate what's been happening. If you haven't figured it out, the world is screwed. So screwed I'm ready to knock back an entire bottle of Scotch in one go. We could really use your help."

Christina looks J-Nel up and down. She stares at him until her posture shows some resolve. She takes a step towards him.

"Yes, you're right about my motives for being here. Before my father died, he was tasked with coming here and looking into the spiritual fluctuations going on. Unfortunately, his heart gave out during an intense training regimen that I advised against. He was attempting to claim our clan's power that links to the Lazuli. So, after he died, his mission was passed onto me. I won't tell you any secrets about my clan, but I can tell you I'm not your enemy nor am I your ally. If I see fit to intervene and help, then I will do so at my own discretion."

Christina has his full attention, but he knows without a doubt that she is someone they desperately need. He put his hands in his pockets.

"Listen, the situation is worse than you can imagine. There's an alien packing an immense level of supernatural power, and he is preparing to decimate us. For all we know, he has an army with him. Please, don't wait until it's too late. If we work together now, we might have a shot."

Christina eyes him.

"What about the anomaly my Elders sensed? I believe his name is Desmond. He seems capable of being the sword you need."

J-Nel's resolve falters slightly at the mention of his brother. A miniscule change in his demeanor, but

Christina still noticed it. J-Nel's voice cracks a little as he stares at the floor.

"Desmond is dead."

Christina stares at him as if she's trying to figure out if he's lying, but she can feel in her gut that what he says is true.

"I'm sorry for your loss. I can sense how much he meant to you."

J-Nel keeps his eyes on the floor.

Christina glances around the room.

"I get it. You guys are in a tight spot; your heaviest hitter is gone and now you need someone who can take up the slack. I can't be what you need. Just like you, I have my own loyalties. There is something I may-"

She abruptly stops talking due to an eerie feeling.

Before J-Nel can respond, Christina glares at him and begins to look around the room again. After surveying the room, she forwards her attention back on J-Nel.

"So that's how it is," Christina says with frustration.

J-Nel meets her gaze with confusion.

She continues.

"You weren't able to pull me to your side, so you decide to bring the big guns."

J-Nel looks even more confused.

"What are you talking about?"

Christina holds her hand out with her palm facing him. He looks at it and notices that the center of her palm is glowing with a pale blue light. Not just glowing, but with a symbol he doesn't recognize. The symbol looks like an upside-down crescent with a slash going down the middle of it. Before he can analyze further, he notices her left eye is also glowing with that pale blue light.

In her palm, particles begin to gather as a handle instantly appears that she grasps. J-Nel watches with fascination as she throws it to her right. While hurling in the air, a blade begins to grow from the handle she just threw.

Suddenly, Berengia appears in his energy form. With a shocked expression, Berengia watches as the now fully formed dagger penetrates his forehead and plunges into the wall behind him.

Berengia steps out of the way to look at the weapon that was meant to kill him. The hilt looks to be made of light blue scales with a guard that curls towards the blade. There is a glowing gemstone embedded in the guard that also gives off a pale blue light.

The dagger dematerializes and reappears in Christina's right hand. Simultaneously, another dagger materializes in her left hand that she aims at J-Nel's throat.

With disgust in her voice, she exclaims, "You must be Berengia."

She cuts her eyes at J-Nel as she continues.

"If this is who your faith is in, then I suggest you go ahead and get your funeral planned. Higher beings such as this one could care less about the humans he toys with."

She sends her cold eyes to Berengia again.

"I know all about you. My clan makes it a point to educate every generation about the so called 'blessings' your kind dish out. Let me ask, oh mighty one. Did you ever think to investigate if any of your charges survived? Did your warriors that you called the Savior's Fist mean anything to you? If they did, you would have known that one survived and that because of her resolve, the clan is what it is today. Whatever is happening, karma is coming to collect."

Berengia begins to defend himself, but a pressure in the room halts his voice. He can sense a dangerous presence around Christina that gives him pause. Visible to only himself, he sees a vague image of an Azure dragon spirit. It looks at him menacingly. Just as quickly as it appeared, it disappears from his line of sight.

Without any hesitation, she twirls her left dagger and knocks J-Nel across his face with the handle. He crumbles to the floor. Both of her daggers dematerialize as she aims both of her pointer fingers at one of the shuttered windows. The tips of those fingers glow, which makes her daggers materialize in front of the metal shutters. With a quick gesture, she makes her daggers carve a large hole that she uses to make her escape out of the office.

J-Nel slowly stands up and gapes at the hole that was made into the shutter. He looks at Berengia who appears to be in shock. Berengia then looks at him as if he's just noticing J-Nel is in the room.

"I came here because I sensed a familiar power. I didn't imagine this power was something I created long ago."

J-Nel scoffs at him.

"Well, I guess now I know I was correct at how dirty your hands are. Desmond wasn't your first or only victim."

Berengia looks away and speaks with regret in his voice.

"I only came here because I wanted to make things right."

J-Nel now looks furious.

"You can't make it right! Whatever cosmic war that your kind are playing with does nothing but make countless victims in the crossfires. Christina's clan dates so far back, that it makes me sick to think you've been making so-called mistakes for that long. You want to make things right? Try doing something useful."

J-Nel narrows his eyes at him.

"It must be nice not to have a physical body and be safe from whatever is coming."

J-Nel taps his watch that makes all the shutters in the room retract. Without another word, J-Nel storms out, leaving Berengia alone in his shame. Berengia looks up with a pained expression just before his body disperses.

Mental Data Entry:

Ten

Well, well, well. It looks like a failure from his past has come back to bite him. I remember that group of humans. They were Berengia's first run at creating elevated beings. Not on the same scale as Desmond, but they were a force to be reckoned with. Too bad Berengia lacked the experience to properly train them. They got slaughtered in the worst way.

Chapter Seventeen:

Level Up

Doctor Edward Williams has always prided himself when it comes to his profession. He has worked hard to build up the reputation he has today. Many in the scientific community would say he is a model of what a humble genius should hope to be in the future. He has always shown nothing but exuberant class.

Today, however, is not a day for a scientific gentleman. As a matter of fact, ever since J-Nel recruited him, Doctor Williams has seemingly been off his leash. He is currently standing in one of SAGA's labs with a childish grin on his face, staring intently at Karina's orange striped fingernails. He can hear Karina and Kelly argue, but he can't seem to care about their squabble. The only thing he can focus on is the golden prize before him. While the ladies continue their debate, he holds Karina's right hand with such reverence.

"This is insane, Karina. I will admit that your 'project' is something to be proud of, but I just can't justify a half a million-dollar price tag on it. A price that I didn't authorize or even know about. I've been looking at your nails for weeks and wondering why the sudden interest in nail artistry. Well, now I know," Kelly says with mock amusement.

Karina sighs deeply as she pinches the bridge of her nose with her free left hand. She looks back at Kelly.

"I'm sorry I didn't tell you, but I wanted to be sure this can be a definite win. Yes, it's expensive as hell, but we need any edge we can get with everything going on. If the doctor here can help me work out the kinks, then it'll be worth it."

Kelly interrupts her logic.

"You're right, we do need every edge. You need to also acknowledge that you could've perfected your 'project' a lot sooner had you simply tuned me into it."

Karina squints her eyes at her.

"That's what this is about? You're not mad about the money at all. This is turning into an argument because I was able to sneak one by you."

Kelly says nothing. Karina simply shakes her head as the realization sinks in.

"Ok, boss. Message received. If you weren't always mean about it, your overprotective big sister nature would almost be touching. Now, let's see what Doctor Williams can make of this."

They both look to him now. He looks up from her nails and holds up a tablet to them.

"The forty-five minutes you two spent bickering, I managed to perform a complete diagnostic on your nanite project. You and your team had a great first start, but I figured out what it lacks."

Karina raises an eyebrow at that. Doctor Williams releases her hand and continues.

"Your team managed to combine organic materials with the nanites to establish a bond with you. Not just any material, though, but with your unique genetic make-up. The nanites were meant to be able to communicate with you on a molecular level, but it seems they lacked the technology to do so. Instead, it appears it will react to your intentions. It's like if you imagine in your head that you want an apple, and then an apple is created just for you. This is something that will take time and focus until you can master it."

Karina looks at her nails with new eyes.

"So, when I was changing the designs, that was an act of intent that I was directing to the nanites?"

Doctor Williams claps his hands together with enthusiasm.

"Precisely! When J-Nel called them Symbiotic Nanites, he was right on the money with that one. Even though you and the nanites cannot directly communicate, they understand what you need in the moment. I'm curious... Were the implants on your occipital bone painful?"

Kelly slowly turns her head towards Karina and questions her with a venomous tone.

"What implants is he talking about, Karina?"

Karina avoids her gaze and answers Doctor Williams quietly.

"No, Doctor Williams, the procedure was done while I was sedated and the nanites helped greatly with the recovery time. Now, I think we should hold off on any more questions." More quietly she adds, "At least until Kelly isn't in the room."

Karina walks to the center of the room and extends her arms in front of her.

"So far, changing nail designs are the only thing I've managed to do by accident, but now that I have an idea on how this works, let's see if I can do it on purpose."

She stares at her nails with a smoldering intensity.

Nothing happens.

She squints her eyes at her nails as if they hold all of life's secrets.

Nothing happens.

She tries looking at them with love in her eyes as if she's a proud parent.

Still, nothing happens.

Karina throws up her hands in annoyance.

"Damnit!"

Doctor Williams approaches her and places his hands on her shoulders.

"Calm down and take a breath."

With a lot of agitation in her posture, she reluctantly does as he asks.

"You are thinking too much on the process. Yes, the nanites you possess are a weapon that were made to do your bidding, but because of the nature of how they were created, you can't think of them in that way. They are an extension of you. Imagine a phantom limb, if you will. That limb is one with you and will perform as intended, but you must treat it like it's a part of you. Relax your mind and seek out your connection with your nanites."

Doctor Williams walks back over to stand next to Kelly. Karina stares at him for a long moment before she refocuses on her nails.

She closes her eyes and lets her arms fall to her side. Doctor Williams grins with anticipation. Kelly has her arms crossed with a hesitant, yet hopeful expression in her eyes.

Karina stands relaxed as she regulates her breathing until it feels as if the air around her has gone completely still.

Without making any sudden movements, she feels a tingly sensation travel through her spine and into her brain. Simultaneously, the same sensation travels in reverse through her legs and feet. Without missing a beat, that same sensation travels once again in reverse through her arms and hands. Instantly, she can feel that sensation coursing through her entire body in perfect synchronization. She opens her eyes as she looks at her nails.

Kelly and Doctor Williams rush over to have a look. Her nails are still green, but now, the color ripples as it instantly changes to orange. It ripples again and changes to a striped design with yellow and red. It ripples again and changes to all black with embedded blue gemstones.

Kelly gasps in surprise.

Doctor Williams yelps with excitement.

Karina can only stare at her nails with astonishment. She looks at Doctor Williams with gratitude.

"Thank you so much for your help, Doctor."

Doctor Williams nods his head with approval.

"It is an honor, I assure you. That was just your first hurdle. Now we must work even harder to make this into an advantage for the battlefield."

Kelly nods in agreement.

Meanwhile, in one of the neighboring training rooms, Timulus and Vyncent are standing silently. Vyncent has his aura present. His energy is flowing off his skin in gentle waves as he breathes with a relaxed posture. Very slowly, all his muscles bulge and expand by three inches. It is a sight to see.

Normally, Vyncent's body structure is built like a lean teenager before puberty. With this transformation, his big head now matches the new bulk of his body.

Vyncent opens his eyes.

"What do you think?"

Timulus circles him while examining him closely. Once he is facing Vyncent again, he answers him.

"You have potential. Your spiritual awareness fluctuates differently than Desmond's, but not in a bad way. The temporary transformative state of your body is also interesting. I would expect a strain on your body or for it to decline when you're not powered up, but it's as if your power knows how to not damage it. Your Spirit Energy doesn't flow internally but externally. That's why you have difficulty using your power at will."

Vyncent gapes at him, but Timulus continues.

"Desmond was teaching you how to be in tune with your inner core because that's how his power functions. Yours requires you to be in tune with your outer body instead. This is very intriguing."

Vyncent releases his hold on his aura just as his body returns to normal. Timulus meets his gaze.

"This explains everything," Vyncent says with enthusiasm. "I've always been self-conscious about my body, so it makes sense this is how I can train to control it more."

Timulus shakes his head.

"Not exactly. Your personal issues with yourself didn't cause this anomaly. The machine Kelly used on you forced your spiritual potential to the surface which made it manifest in a bizarre structure. This is because the machine didn't know how to properly guide your core for elevation. Remember, Vyncent, every living being has spiritual potential inside of them. Unfortunately, yours was snatched out prematurely instead of you becoming one with it. You may not look the part, but even when your power isn't fully active, your body can perform well on its own."

Before Vyncent can question what Timulus meant by that, Timulus rushes him and throws a punch. By using his focused reaction ability, he catches Timulus' fist, but he takes a step back in the process.

Timulus nods appraisingly at him.

"We must train your mind to be in sync with your body, so you can elevate physically with your power. We can't make you a combat genius overnight, but we can improve your battle instincts."

Vyncent gulps.

"Alright. Let's do this."

Chapter Eighteen: Guidance

Christina is pacing within the living room of her log cabin. She mutters to herself with a quizzical expression on her face. What's troubling her is the interaction she had with J-Nel the other day. She's very good at reading people and it is no surprise that she knows he comes from a genuine state of mind.

The problem is that it seems he is in league with that false-faced, backstabbing, cowardly child of a higher being. Her clan has engraved her mind into not trusting that apparition, but it's not Berengia that pleaded for her help. It was a man who is in desperate need of help to save the world. She knows that if she joins them, their chances of survival will greatly increase. The challenge, though, is convincing the Elders that her help is the right move here.

The Elders aren't cruel people. They just don't want their agents going into battle unnecessarily. The

Lazuli has made outstanding efforts to remain a mystery to the outside world, and joining this battle would attract curious eyes. If she can assure them that she can stay out of the limelight, then surely, they'll allow her to fight.

She stops pacing abruptly and stares off into the distance.

"Who am I kidding? Even if they say no, I'll just go off and do my own thing as usual."

With her mind made up, she turns around and stares at the palms of her hands. The symbol of the Lazuli glows with its pale blue light. She stretches her hands in front of herself with focus and concentration. Within seconds, the symbol glows more intensely when she gives a command.

"Lazuli Gate!"

A door-shaped portal appears in front of her that gives off an aura of the same pale blue light that she also is blanketed with.

From her position, she can clearly see what's on the other side. There are two stone pillars attached to an arc that is twenty-five feet wide. There are four guards standing at that gateway with two of them armed with dual swords and the remaining armed with long spears. The handles on all the weapons have the same dragon scale texture as Christina's daggers, but without a gem embedded into the guards or handles. Their surroundings are lush greenery that rivals the most beautiful jungles in the world.

At first glance you can see silky oak trees, pitcher plants, acai trees, bougainvillea plants, carnauba trees, and off to the sides you can see glimpses of Amazonian water lilies. Christina knows there is much more to be seen, but the first impression from the portal is always a beautiful sight.

The second she steps into the portal and arrives on the other side, it closes behind her. The guards all give her a respectful nod as she walks through.

The first thing to notice inside this compound is the lively activity. The people who choose to live here have adopted a simple yet fulfilling lifestyle. There is an abundance of stalls that offer goods such as meat, vegetables, and other household items that are essential.

The Lazuli Village is such a rich place that the residents here provide their products for free, simply because they enjoy the work that they can provide. The village has no need for profit or any existence for monopoly. Each time Christina can visit her home, she smiles with pride because she knows that this place is the most peaceful to ever exist.

She chuckles inside at that same notion, because if anyone ever tried to conquer their lands, even the children here would be able to stop them.

After walking through what people would see as a plaza, she is able to see the grand structure known as the Lazuli Temple. As she ventures inside, she is surprised that only one of the Elders is waiting for her.

This individual is a Caucasian female with auburn hair and green eyes.

"Christina, I felt your aura screaming with determination before you even opened your Ka Gate to get here," Jade says with a grin.

Christina looks around with confusion.

"I expected all the Elders to be here to talk me out of my line of logic."

Jade simply smiles as she walks towards Christina and takes her hands. She looks deeply into Christina's eyes.

"They have been using their gifted sight to watch over this journey you have taken. The fact that your father took an interest in Seredia Island spoke volumes when you decided to pick up where he left off. They see the danger. They can feel the destruction the world will take if you don't join this war."

Christina looks at her suspiciously.

"I highly doubt they gave me their blessings from the kindness of their hearts."

Jade gives her a mischievous grin.

"Well, it's not my fault that my voice has more weight when it comes to those old fools. Before your grandmother left this world, she made sure my presence held as much value as her own. So yes, as your mother and a member of the Elder Tribe, I fought for your right to choose how to perceive this incoming threat."

Jade holds Christina at arms lengths as she continues.

"I'm so very proud of you, Chrissy. Your father would be too. I want you to go out there and show those novice's how it's done."

Christina crushes her mother with a bear hug and releases her.

"Thank you. I'll do my best."

Jade fights back the tears welling in her eyes.

"Your best is always top notch, my little pin prick."

Christina rolls her eyes.

"You're never going to let that nickname go. One time. I only once used your pins from your sewing kit as pretend throwing knives to practice with."

Jade chuckles.

"Your father's thigh would argue it wasn't your finest moment."

They both laugh at the memory.

Chapter Nineteen:
Lazuli History

The Elders of the Lazuli Clan are not all old people. The term 'Elder' was only used because this group of individuals have the clan's best interest truly at heart. To have a position among the Elders is the greatest honor a clan person may hope to achieve. This is due to the fact that members of the Elders are chosen by the Lazuli Spirit herself. The blessing from the Lazuli isn't limited to the access of her power; it also comes with the gift of life longevity.

The Lazuli Spirit was once human. During her mortal life, she was known as Maya. She originated from the Great Demon War and was also a member of the infamous Savior's Fist.

Through her own determination, Maya survived the worst of the war and became the only survivor of the Savior's Fist.

When Berengia initially bestowed upon her the blessing, she could only channel her body to the peak of human perfection. She gained the strength of a thousand men, speed that put the entire cheetah species to shame, eyes sharper than the mightiest falcon, and wisdom that outshined the greatest scholars. Those gifts, unfortunately, did not give her and her friends the means to survive the war.

It was nearly a decade later that her inert power started to evolve into what Christina can do today. Her power was considered Spirit Energy, but was vastly different than what Berengia intended to create for the humans. Maya decided to name this power Dragon's Pulse.'

At the time, she didn't know why that name resonated with her, but she knew it was meant to be. This evolved power allowed her soul to bond with a weapon and increase her already heightened human senses. The weapon that she bonded with was also elevated to match her own strength in terms of durability and the ability to manipulate it telepathically.

After founding the clan and sharing her beliefs, she found herself able to unlock cores within others so they could wield the same strength she has. Maya soon discovered that although her clan people could reach the peak of human perfection, they couldn't, however, use the Dragon's Pulse.

Maya lived to be two-hundred and twelve years old. She devoted her life to creating a peaceful community with the means of defending themselves and helping the outside world when needed. The day she passed is a day the clan celebrates to this day.

The moment she took her final breath, her entire body released a massive surge of energy. At first, the energy flooded her people with empowerment and enriched the soils of their lands.

But then, the energy collected itself into the air above the village and started to take form. The clan people gazed in wonder as the energy transformed into what they know now as the Lazuli Dragon Spirit.

Immediately, Maya knew what her life had become. She knew at that moment that she would be able to guide her clan for as long as needed. Just as she realized this, she chose her first successor among the clan people and bonded her spirit with that person, making them the first in the clan's history to wield the Dragon's Pulse.

Chapter Twenty:
Duty Calls

Although the Elders could observe Christina with their sight, they are not able to capture the entire journey. For instance, they cannot hear her thoughts or experience what impacted her in those moments. In the early days, the sight used to only provide grainy images, but now it's like their minds can broadcast in 4K resolution.

The only drawback, though, is that the target must be a willing participant to make observing easier. A target who doesn't want to be viewed takes a lot more energy to look upon.

After a few hours of retelling her adventures on Seredia Island, Christina and Jade both laugh at how funny life has become.

"What was that boy's name? Vyncent! That's his name. I wish I could've witnessed his reaction when that axe almost took his head."

Christina wipes a tear from her eye.

"It was priceless. I knew they were there, but I wanted to have a little fun with them."

Jade looks up with a thoughtful expression.

"It is surprising about that Desmond character."

"Why do you say that?" Christina asks.

Jade looks at her seriously now.

"The moment he acquired his power is when he made his mark on the Spectrum."

Christina shrugs.

"I know it's part of our teachings, but come on, Mother. Even you must admit it's crazy to believe that our universe is a fragmented mess."

Jade shakes her head.

"You are the only member other than the Lazuli mother herself who has seen Berengia in person. You watched Vyncent and those aliens fight with abilities that were thought to be impossible to have. Those events alone strengthen my belief that the Spectrum is real."

Christina still isn't convinced, but her mother continues.

"Come now, the fact that our village exists in a pocket dimension should be proof enough for you. Anyway, as far as that man, Desmond. When us Elders used our foresight, it was clear that he would become the start of what the Spectrum needs. We witnessed possible futures of what he was meant to accomplish."

Christina interrupts.

"Key word here is possible. As great as the Elders' foresight can be, it can't predict everything."

Her expression becomes more somber with her next words.

"It couldn't even see that Dad was going to die."

Christina and Jade become silent with grief.

Jade is about to say something comforting, but she hesitates as she looks off into the distance. She forwards her attention to the sky. Christina notices, but before she can inquire, Jade's eyes turn completely white, and her body begins to tremble. Christina knows better than to touch her.

"Mom! What is it?"

Jade's eyes return to normal as she slowly focuses on Christina.

"That alien has played with the fabric of reality with no concern for the consequences. You need to go back. Now. Focus on the one that gave you a hard time. J-Nel is his name, right?"

Christina shakes her head.

"I've never used the Ka Gate to single out a person before. Only a destination."

Jade abruptly stands up and guides Christina to her feet. She grabs Christina's left hand.

"Trust me. It will be a lot easier than traveling here. You two may not be close, but you still formed a connection with him that will allow you to trace his location. Focus on the Dragon's Pulse and command your link to J-Nel."

Christina flexes her arm and focuses on her power as the symbol on her right palm glows. She stares into the air before her.

Chapter Twenty-One:
It's About To Go Down

J-Nel is standing with Kelly in an observation deck that is stationed above the training room. The room itself is built with an octagon structure as well as glass walls and flooring. The glass is military grade that could withstand a couple hits from rocket launchers before showing signs of giving way. They both look down at Karina and Vyncent as they spar with one another.

Kelly has been observing them with a decent amount of respect. In the short time that Timulus has been guiding him, Vyncent has improved a great deal now that he understands his power more.

Karina, on the other hand, impressed Kelly on a fundamental level. Not only is she wielding advanced tech this world hasn't seen yet, but she operates it with such grace and ferociousness. She understands this proudness is biased, but she can't help it.

Karina was right before; Kelly has always approached Karina with a big sister protectiveness. She can't explain why that is, though. Before Desmond and Karina came under her wing, she had made a point to never play favorites or get on any emotional level with her agents, but look at her now.

She may refer to most of them by their agent assigned number, but inside she knows them all by name. She has internal knowledge whether they have families or not. Some may consider it a breach of privacy, but she also keeps up with her agent's financial lives. If there is an injustice from greedy bill collectors, she will step in and help those bloodsuckers reconsider their next move.

Take Janice, for instance. Agent three-six-one. She is currently on maternity leave, and she has about two weeks until she is bound to return to work. Kelly not only sent an anonymous care package for the baby, but she also made sure that Janice will return to work with a bonus, a promotion with a desk job, and a set of new hours that will give her more time with her baby. If she was married, Kelly wouldn't have gone to such lengths, but she doesn't trust that boyfriend of Janice's to step up to the plate. He can barely keep his job at the grocery store.

While Kelly has been in deep thought, J-Nel has been talking to her this entire time. She didn't start tuning in until he mentioned something about the Lazuli Clan. She turns to him.

"You know about the Lazuli? I don't mean to sound so surprised, but that clan has made it almost impossible for anyone to learn about them."

J-Nel shrugs.

"I get it. Remember that girl I told you about?"

Kelly nods her head.

J-Nel strokes his goatee as he continues.

"She's a clan member."

Kelly perks up at that information and focuses her full attention on him.

J-Nel smirks.

"I know what you're thinking. Yes, she would be a very big asset with this war we're in. Unfortunately, she's made it very clear that she is not here to solve our problems."

Kelly's excitement dissipates.

"That's a shame. We could have learned a lot from her. Oh well."

Kelly takes out a belt buckle from her pocket and hands it to J-Nel.

"What's this?"

Without looking at him she explains, "Put that on your belt. If you find yourself in a tight jam, press the center to activate a large energy field. I know you have your kinetic bands, but I also remember they have limits. That device will summon a force field in front of you and will stay there until whatever force breaks it. It is meant to buy you time or to take a hit you're not sure your bands can handle."

J-Nel looks at her with surprise.

"Thank you. I'll admit this is unexpected."

"Jason, you four are about to go into a battle of titans. You are more fragile than they are. I mean this with no disrespect, but I wanted to at least do my part to make sure you are properly equipped. You are a born leader. Outside of myself, you do a great job at keeping them focused and encouraged. I don't want to see you die out there."

Before he can fully process what she said, his attention shifts to Doctor Williams. His face has become flushed while staring at his screen.

Kelly follows his gaze.

J-Nel grabs his trench coat from a chair and skillfully throws it on in a single fluid motion. They both turn and enter the teleportation pad that instantly moves them to the ground level of the training room. While heading towards Doctor Williams, he notices them approaching. As soon as J-Nel and Kelly are within earshot, Doctor Williams begins stammering.

"When I first stumbled on the doorway to what we now know as the mirrored dimension, I've been studying its energy signatures. They are unique. Nothing in this world is even closely related to it."

J-Nel interrupts him.

"Get to the point please."

"Right," Doctor Williams says bashfully. "Well, the energy signature vanished."

The air suddenly becomes still.

"Where did it go? It had to have gone somewhere," Kelly says.

Doctor Williams slowly rises from his chair while still staring at the computer screen.

"The doorway is right out front of SAGA Headquarters now."

J-Nel and Kelly appear shocked by his news.

Before either of them can respond, an alarm begins to blare throughout the entire headquarters. A computerized voice begins an announcement.

"All personnel, gear up and arm yourselves. This is not a test or drill. An unknown entity is within threatening parameters of the headquarters. I repeat, this is not a test or drill. All non-combatant agents please head towards your nearest panic room location."

Karina and Vyncent joined J-Nel and Kelly during the announcement. Hologram feeds appear in the room that shows the doorway is exactly where Doctor Williams said it is. This time it is more pronounced and intimidating. Its size matches a three-bedroom apartment. Timulus is already outside staring at the doorway in the middle of the bridge. He is showing no fear as he stands ready with his fist clenched and aura flaring.

"Get out there and back him up. I'll coordinate my agents and monitor things from here," Kelly commands.

Without hesitation, J-Nel, Karina, and Vyncent enter a teleportation pad that instantly sends them to the front door. They all run to join Timulus.

"I don't see how you people can use those pads so frequently without your molecules becoming unstable," J-Nel says with some unease in his voice.

"It helps when we have some of the best scientists and mathematicians on payroll," Karina responds while keeping her gaze ahead.

Within a moment, they all have reached Timulus' side and join him to stare at the doorway.

"Doorways to dimensions have never been documented to move before. Once they're in a hotspot, that's where they stay until closed or reopened," Timulus says gravely.

The doorway pulses twice which makes them all tense up.

J-Nel activates his kinetic bands just as he takes out a laser sword and gun.

Vyncent forms his aura, which also activates his muscles to expand.

Karina simply gets into a fighting stance, but her nails are noticeably glistening.

Fraq, Rei, and Skuzy fly out of the doorway and land mere yards away from the group. Fraq takes a few steps forward with a cocky grin.

"I'll be honest, humans. After hearing about Desmond being dead, I expected no fight at all. It appears I was solely mistaken with all your preparations and training."

J-Nel takes a step forward.

"This is your only chance to give this up before we demolish you."

J-Nel knew this was an empty bluff, but he had to try regardless. Besides, it's three versus four right now. He's sure they can at least handle those odds.

Without another word, six more Plutonian soldiers fly out of the doorway to join their companions' sides.

J-Nel almost wishes he hadn't said anything.

Fraq chuckles.

"Our only chance, huh? After you all are out of the way, Czar will drain Berengia dry and take from him what he needs to become a god. We will reap the rewards as he takes this world and countless others."

A gunshot is heard, but Fraq reacts by using his armored hand to deflect the bullet.

"You talk too much," J-Nel says mockingly.

Fraq glares at him, but then he feels an unusual sensation. He looks at his armored hand and notices that the bullet is lodged into it. An explosion comes from the bullet that tears apart the armor surrounding his hand sending small bits of shrapnel into his face. After the smoke clears, his hand looks as if it had been mauled and his face has many cuts on it. He glares at J-Nel and speaks with a furious tone.

"Kill them all! Leave that one to me."

Timulus kicks off by charging first with a low war cry. His intentions were to face Fraq before he got to J-Nel, but two of his lackeys intercepted him. One of the soldiers creates a pair of combat canes with curved and sharpened ends. His other opponent creates a large battle axe that he wields and twirls with ease. The axe soldier intervenes first by swinging his axe downward, but Timulus easily dodges.

The axe soldier grins.

Before Timulus can ponder on that bizarre expression, the curve of a cane latches onto his left wrist. Without a second to react, the cane soldier uses the momentum to slam Timulus face-first to the ground. The axe soldier dashes forward and begins to swing downward, but another bullet is lodged into the blade of the axe. An explosion occurs that sends his swing off target.

The axe soldier glares at J-Nel who gives him a cocky grin.

Timulus uses the opportunity to punch the cane soldier and follows up by kicking the axe soldier in the face. With all of them on their feet, a standoff happens. Within a second, they attack each other fiercely with Timulus blocking and countering their movements.

Two more soldiers charge forward, but this time, Vyncent is the one to act. His aura flares more as he strikes fist-to-fist with one of them. A small shockwave occurs from the connecting blow.

Vyncent unfurls a fist and grasps his opponent's wrist. Without giving the Plutonian time to react, Vyncent pulls him in closer and uppercuts him deep in the stomach. The Plutonian soldier's breath is knocked right out of him.

Vyncent releases him and jumps into the air to kick him to the ground. He grounds himself immediately after the attack. The other soldier creates a scythe and lunges towards Vyncent with a determined expression. The scythe soldier swings wide, but Vyncent uses his focused reaction ability to estimate the strike.

By reflex, Vyncent reinforces his aura on his forearm to block the attack and follows up by kicking the scythe soldier in the chest, which sends him spiraling a yard away.

The other soldier regains his footing as he creates a broadsword with Spirit Energy coming off it like a flame. He dashes forward and attacks Vyncent with a flurry of strikes.

By using his focused reaction ability, Vyncent can easily dodge the attacks. Unfortunately, he doesn't see the scythe soldier sneaking up behind him with his weapon raised.

Before the soldier can make a move, an energy blast hits him on the ankle which causes him to flip and land face-first on the ground.

Karina has her arm outstretched with her right fist facing that direction. She took a page out of the boys' book to have her energy attacks be controlled through a fisted trigger. Her nanite armor is currently covering her hand and arm up to her elbow.

From what can be seen, the armor is giving off a metallic version of the color amaranth. It has a beautiful reddish-pink hue.

She glares at the scythe soldier as her armor begins to cover her other hand and forearm.

Vyncent nods at her with appreciation.

Without wasting any time, he deflects a broadsword strike and headbutts the soldier. Vyncent uses the chance to sweep the soldier's legs, which causes him to fall straight onto his back.

Vyncent immediately does a backflip and lands his knee onto the back of the scythe soldier. The scythe soldier yells out in pain as blood spurts out of his mouth.

Karina's armor envelops her entire body, leaving only her face visible and her hair spilling out of the back in a ponytail. Her entire new uniform that is her nanite armor is the color amaranth. Her hands and forearms are expanded into white gauntlets that maintain a metallic appearance as well as her feet and calves. The word SAGA is etched into the left shoulder with the same white texture. There are also two orbs that are protruding from her back that share the white texture.

I'll think of this model as Paragon 1.0. I'm sure I'll run through many different designs, Karina thinks.

The remaining two lackeys take notice of Karina's transformation and decide to engage her. Before they get halfway, the orbs on her back begin to glow and erupt a controlled amount of energy that propels her to fly into the soldier's direction.

As they head in each other's direction, one of the soldiers creates a macuahuitl. A wooden club with several embedded Seredium blades.

The other soldier creates a pair of chakrams that have wicked and jagged blades. It also has a handle for a grip. The chakrams do not connect full circle.

Karina's gauntlets ripple and extend a two-foot blade on each arm that jets out past her hands. She collides with the macuahuitl soldier creating a stalemate. She uses her free arm to bring up a blade that cuts the soldier across his chest. He grunts in pain and forcibly backs away from her. She cuts her eyes to her left and deflects a chakram flying her way. The chakram stops in midair while still spinning before it goes straight back to its owner.

The chakram soldier catches it with ease while still dashing towards Karina.

She engages him and they begin to trade blow for blow. The chakram soldier allows her blades to go through his rings so he could twist and lock her in.

From above, the macuahuitl soldier brings his sword down to cut her in half. Karina smirks as she retracts her blades to free herself and follows up by using her orbs to move backwards.

The macuahuitl hits the ground with so much force that it causes a slight tremor and multiple cracks into the concrete. He looks in Karina's direction to see that her hands have transformed into energy cannons. She grins as she fires off a blast point blank into his face that sends him skidding across the ground.

The chakram soldier watches as his comrade is sent hurling like a ragdoll. He gazes at Karina in fear. Her grin fades as she closes the distance and sucker punches him to the ground. He lays there sprawled out and unconscious.

Nearby, Vyncent has just punched the broadsword soldier's Soul Pack hard enough to cause it to rupture. Consequently, a relentless surge of energy electrocutes them both. After a moment, the energy is exhausted and the soldier collapses to the ground in a heap. Vyncent was able to catch his balance on one knee to prevent himself from blacking out. The same can't be said for the broadsword soldier. He breathes hard as he looks over at the scythe soldier who still hasn't gotten up from Vyncent's last attack.

Timulus has just caught the blade of an axe so he can push the soldier away from him. The cane soldier rushes in, but Timulus raises a fist and blasts him directly in the face. The cane soldier falls backwards and hits his head hard on the ground.

Timulus turns around to see the axe soldier swing at him. His axe digs into Timulus' chest. The soldier smiles with glee, but it fades when he realizes there's no blood. The blade only cut into Timulus' Spirit Energy and not flesh. With a grunt, Timulus flares his Spirit Energy to push the soldier away from him once again.

As soon as the soldier is stumbling, Timulus opens his palms to release a mass of energy that engulfs the soldier. The energy is so potent that it disintegrates his opponent.

He breathes heavily from exertion, but he controls it and walks over to stand with the others.

Fraq has watched this battle with a disbelieving expression.

Rei and Skuzy exchange a look.

Fraq clutches his fist and begins to walk in their direction. His Soul Pack powers to life as Spirit Energy begins to blaze off him like an inferno. His eyes become deranged, and his hair seems to flow with a wild pattern.

He forms a colossal sword in one hand and a large, spiked mace in the other.

"I am sick of you humans making a mockery of Czar's will. They may not have been a challenge, but I will destroy each of you right here. I will make you beg for mercy! I will make a stew of your blood and shattered bones when my victory comes. Sip it like fine wine as your world burns to ashes."

Before he can utter another word, a dagger materializes behind him and penetrates his skull. He comes to a halt to process what just happened. The dagger pulls back and twirls around to slice his throat open. It then strikes him through the chest and exits from the other side. Fraq falls face-first to the ground.

He's dead.

The dagger then sails through the air past the group. They follow the dagger with their eyes to see it land in the hand of Christina who is walking out of her Ka Gate. It closes immediately once she is fully out of it.

"J-Nel is right," Christina says with a bored tone. "You talk way too much."

Above them, the doorway pulses three times. J-Nel looks at Christina with surprise.

"I thought you weren't an ally?"

Christina smirks.

"I thought you could use some muscle, but it looks like you all have things under control."

Karina approaches Christina.

"We can use all the help we can get. I'll wager that was just the welcoming wagon."

Christina nods and looks to Rei and Skuzy who haven't moved an inch. Timulus steps forward to address them.

"Are you two just going to watch or will we have to mow you down as well?"

Rei and Skuzy exchange another look, but it's Rei who decides to speak up.

"We weren't sure if you all were up to the task, but it's clear it was smart of us to hold out. You don't know this Timulus, but we were part of Berengia's Arcane Guard."

Timulus physically looks surprised by this news.

"His Arcane Guard? You two were talked about as if you were a myth. No one knew your identities, yet you can easily carry out any task unseen."

Rei nods her head in agreement.

"That is correct. Even in the face of Montezuma's attack, we were able to evacuate children and other important officials to a safe location. As far as we know, our targets are still safe. Listen carefully, Czar has been watching your movements since Vyncent over there had his first run in with Fraq. And the way the doorway is pulsing, it means Czar is getting closer to his endgame. You all need to get in there and do what you need to do.

We'll stand guard here and make sure to put down any Plutonian soldier that comes through."

They all gape at her until J-Nel breaks the silence.

"How do we know you're telling the truth?"

Berengia appears between the two groups. He looks at the girls and back at the humans. He is instantly met with hostile eyes from the group. He looks each of them in the eye.

"I can confirm that they are truly my Arcane Guard."

J-Nel and Christina scoff at his statement.

Timulus steps forward and looks at Berengia.

"I believe I can speak for everyone here that our trust in you is still very fragile. If you are here to help, then now is your chance to start earning some of that trust back."

Berengia nods as if he had just come to a decision.

"I will remain here with my guard and use my own energy to reinforce theirs."

No one understands the implications here, except for Timulus who looks at him surprisingly. He turns to his friends and explains.

"If he means what he says, then he will be taking a risk. Reinforcing not just one, but two people's Spirit

Energy will eat away at his own life force. By taking this action, regaining our trust is genuine."

No one says a word, but even Christina looks impressed.

J-Nel steps in front of his group.

"Listen guys, we don't know what we will find out there, but we cannot allow Czar to live. He has plans and we need to disrupt them by any means necessary. Are you with me?"

Everyone nods their heads in agreement.

"Then let's go to work."

Timulus and Vyncent take flight and throw themselves into the doorway.

Karina activates her orbs while taking hold of J-Nel so they both can enter.

Before Christina takes a step, she approaches Berengia warily. She looks at him up and down. Berengia meets her gaze and notices that one of her eyes has a twinkle of pale blue light.

"I am Maya's twenty-third successor. Throughout history, it seems that I am one of the few she fully resonated with. She has a message for you."

Berengia looks at her unblinking. She continues.

"She forgave you a long time ago. She even understands that your upbringing is what caused you to make a lot of mistakes. She, at times, pities the loneliness you must feel throughout your long life. She holds no ill will, but there needs to be an understanding."

Christina crosses her arms.

"Right here is your one chance to become greater than you have been. Screw us over and she promises to take full control of my body to give you a reckoning. A sacrifice I'm willing to make to allow her to put you down for good. Make no mistake, oh mighty one, she has become strong enough to make good on it."

Without waiting for a reply, she activates her power and jumps high into the air to enter the doorway.

Berengia takes a moment to look at the doorway before he glances at the SAGA building.

"I know you heard everything. I'm also sure you have a lot of weapons trained on me, but you should know that you'll be wasting your ammo. I can't take any physical damage in this form. Can we call a truce for now, Kelly?"

The main doors of SAGA open. A group of fifty agents pour out as they flank Berengia on both sides. They don't aim their guns at him, but at the doorway to the mirrored dimension. Berengia nods his head and decides to take that as an agreement to a truce. He does wonder just what counter measures she would really plan to use on him.

Agent zero-four-six approaches him.

"Boss wants to know the plan and how can we help."

Skuzy steps in to provide an answer.

"As soon as the others make it to the other side, Czar will send a fleet of soldiers over here. Our job, as well as yours, is to make sure they don't reach the population."

She meets Berengia's gaze and nods. He nods back and addresses the SAGA agent.

"I will be fortifying Rei and Skuzy's power while you all back them up when needed. The line is drawn with us."

The agent salutes and relays the message to the rest of his squad.

Before anyone can ask any more questions, the doorway pulses once. Everyone looks up at it with anticipation.

Berengia's hands glow as he stands with determination. Rei and Skuzy's bodies flare with an intense aura.

"As long as I'm connected, you won't need to use your Soul Packs or need to worry about how much power you're using. Give it all you've got!" Berengia shouts.

A horde of Plutonian soldiers spill out of the doorway. As soon as they jump out, they are already equipped with their weapon of choice.

Skuzy creates her bow and pulls on the string. An arrow made of energy is created as she fires shot after shot. Her aim is so precise that she is consistently doing headshots.

The agents of SAGA all watch her work with disbelieving gazes.

Rei creates a pole axe that has a blade on one end, a steel spike on top, and a hammerhead on the other end. She twirls it around her with ease as she charges for the small army. She clashes with a machete soldier. She parries and slices his throat open. She turns to bash in the skull of another soldier and throws her pole axe at a soldier who is creeping behind Skuzy. The steel pike of the pole axe impales the sneaky soldier through the back of the head.

Skuzy doesn't react to what just happened. She just keeps firing.

The pole axe disperses. Rei creates another one as she continues to spread havoc.

The SAGA agents break out of their staring and join the battle by firing precise shots.

Berengia creates a barrier around himself so his energy output isn't interrupted.

Chapter Twenty-Two: Warriors United

On the other side of the doorway, Karina and Christina find themselves standing near a mirrored version of Seredia Tower.

"It's creepy how quiet it is here," Karina says.

"I once trained in an underground cavern for six months. I was blindfolded the entire time and had my hearing disabled for the first three months. All I could rely on was the vibrations all around me. You wouldn't believe the creatures that I fought who sought the honor of devouring me."

Karina stares at her.

"You really had an interesting life," Karina says with an unsure tone.

Christina shrugs.

"Without that experience, I'm sure this place would have driven me crazy. I'm Christina, by the way."

She offers her hand to Karina who takes it and shakes it.

"I'm Karina. Vyncent mentioned you before, but he left out how much of a badass you are."

Christina glances at her before turning her attention back to their surroundings.

"You're not too bad yourself. I caught some of your fight before I intervened. I'd be open to sparring with you when this is over."

"You're that sure we'll survive this?" Karina asks.

Christina squats down and places her hand on the ground with her eyes closed.

"I can't speak for the boys, but I'm surer about us two."

Christina scrunches her nose as if she smelled a foul odor.

"This place is strange. It's an exact replica of Seredia Island, but that's it. The only thing that exists in this realm is the island."

Karina looks visibly startled by the news.

"Are you sure? Timulus and Doctor Williams seemed convinced that this is a copy of the entire world."

Christina stands up and faces Karina.

"Our world has a system of countless vibrations running through it. This land only has a single network that consists of this Island and nothing else. That alien is up to no good here."

Meanwhile, Timulus has found himself in a darkened corridor. He's not sure how the doorways work, but he feels they shouldn't drop people in random locations. Then again, how would he know for sure?

Most people would struggle to find their way in complete darkness, but Timulus reinforces his eyes with his Spirit Energy. It's not a perfect solution, but it helps to not trip over anything.

He stops suddenly when he hears a voice in the distance. No, not just one voice, but a large group of yelling and laughing. He decides to follow the path that leads him to what he's hearing. He's hoping this will lead him to Czar so he can put an end to this. Berengia said he wasn't strong enough, but who is he to say what Timulus' limits are? Timulus likes to think he knows his own limits well.

After many twists and turns, he can roughly see that he has entered a large room. He stops dead in his tracks. The voices he heard have suddenly become quiet. It's as if his presence in this room has stilled the air.

The lights turn on to reveal a replica of the training room inside SAGA. The difference here is the room has been modified with many rows of bleachers. Timulus estimates at least a hundred of Czar's minions fill those bleachers.

The room erupts in yells and curses now that he can see his surroundings. He looks up to see Czar hovering in the air with his arms folded and a small smile on his face.

Timulus takes notice of how much Czar has bulked up. He now understands the meaning behind the phrase 'tree trunk arms' and 'barrel chest.'

Czar's eyes flash with his red Spirit Energy.

"First one to bring me his head will be next in line as my second in command. Since Fraq is dead, the spot appears to be vacant."

The cheers are so powerful they overwhelm Timulus' ears.

Three soldiers immediately take to the ground floor and slowly approach Timulus. He flares his aura and readies himself in a fighting stance.

One soldier uses his Soul Pack to create dual crossbows. The second creates a sledgehammer. The third one creates a cat o' nine tails whip in one hand and a mace with a bronze head in the other. This soldier is known as the Fanatic.

The crossbow soldier fires two shots in Timulus' direction. Timulus deflects one of the bolts, but he catches the other and hurls it at the sledgehammer soldier who swings his weapon in an arc to deflect it.

Timulus raises a fist and fires two energy blasts at the sledgehammer soldier, but he dodges one and hits the other with his weapon.

After closing the gap, the soldier disperses his weapon and tackles Timulus to the ground. He moves to lock Timulus into a hold, but Timulus reacts quickly by reversing and tossing the soldier away.

The Fanatic closes in and slashes him across his back with his whip, leaving six whelps across his skin. Timulus is surprised the attack was able to penetrate his aura. He turns to counter, but the Fanatic uppercuts him with the mace and cross-kicks him in the face.

Timulus staggers and wipes the blood from his mouth. The Fanatic dashes forward with an overhead swing with his mace, but Timulus catches his forearm and buries his fist in his sternum. Timulus can hear the bones crack as the Fanatic collapses to the ground.

A bolt grazes his cheek which causes him to duck as another bolt sails past his head.

Before he can move in the crossbow soldier's direction, the sledgehammer soldier appears in front of him and hits Timulus on his leg and follows up by taking a step back and hitting him directly in the stomach. Timulus yells out in pain while coughing up blood at the same time.

The sledgehammer soldier attempts another strike, but he can't pull his weapon back. Timulus looks up at him to reveal his hands gripping the pole of the sledgehammer. He grins as he shoves the handle into the soldier's stomach, making him gasp for air.

Timulus backhands him and lands a kick directly on his chin that sends the soldier sprawling on the ground.

Timulus gives the crossbow soldier a death glare. The soldier turns around and runs away.

The surrounding crowd boos the runaway.

From above, a red wave of energy descends onto the fleeing soldier. The energy rips him apart. This makes the crowd erupt in even louder cheers.

For whatever reason, the rest of the crowd has become emboldened enough to leave the bleachers all at once. Timulus doesn't panic though. He prepares himself to fend off his incoming attackers. Timulus' eyes glow brightly, and his Spirit Energy flows around him like a torrent.

Before a punch can be thrown, Timulus releases a sphere of energy that knocks every soldier to the ground. His shoulders sag as he takes in the environment. Every single soldier is unconscious, but it came at a price.

Czar descends to the ground and lands mere feet in front of Timulus. He is no longer smiling.

"You have impressed me, Timulus, but now this won't be a fair fight. You have expended your core."

Timulus stands there breathing hard without the energy to give him a reply.

Czar shakes his head and unfolds his arms as he forms his aura.

"Are you really going to fight a defenseless opponent?" Timulus asks.

Czar grins.

"Timulus, I am not an honorable man. I will kick you while you're down and laugh at your suffering. Don't worry, you're not going to die just yet."

Timulus' eyes bulge as he gasps for air. He looks down to see that Czar's elbow has connected with his stomach.

Czar attacked so rapidly, that when Timulus blinked, he missed the movement.

Czar uppercuts him so hard that a loud crack reverberates throughout the training room. Timulus feels his jawbone crack under the pressure of the attack. Czar roundhouse kicks Timulus in the side of his torso and sends him tumbling on the ground.

Czar's body phases away and reappears to intercept Timulus. Czar kicks him into the air.

While airborne, Timulus realizes that he never had a chance at being a match for Czar.

Meanwhile, J-Nel and Vyncent have found themselves on the bridge that connects the replica SAGA to the island. They both have confused expressions on their faces.

"Are we in the mirrored dimension or are we still in our own?" Vyncent asks.

J-Nel takes a few steps while he looks around.

"Judging from how quiet it is, I think we made it through."

J-Nel faces Vyncent and looks at him with a strange expression. With no warning, he pulls out his gun and aims it at Vyncent.

Vyncent instantly panics and ducks just as J-Nel pulls the trigger. Vyncent straightens up with a furious expression.

"What is wrong with you? Damnit Jason, I thought we made it past your issues with me."

J-Nel looks him in the eye and tilts his head.

"Look behind you."

Vyncent gives him a glare before doing as he asks and notices a dead Plutonian on the ground.

"As I always say, Vyncent, be mindful of your surroundings."

They both look further down the bridge to see a small army of soldiers standing idle. J-Nel readies his laser sword.

"You ready, Vyncent?"

Vyncent levitates slightly in the air as he forms his aura.

"This time, J-Nel, I'm more than ready."

The army of soldiers charge as Vyncent flies towards them. J-Nel runs towards the approaching army with his laser sword and pistol at the ready.

Vyncent punches a soldier, spins around to uppercut another, and thrusts his foot into the jaw of another soldier. Vyncent makes two fists as he rapidly fires energy blasts at surrounding enemies and releases a war cry.

J-Nel decapitates a soldier, guts another, and shoots a soldier twice in the face. He ducks an incoming attack and counters with three bullets to the neck of that soldier.

Another soldier swings wide at him with a katana, but J-Nel manages to sidestep out of the way and counter with his laser sword through the soldier's chest. Another soldier surprises him with a gut punch with spiked brass knuckles.

The brass knuckle soldier grins, but his face falls when he realizes J-Nel is unharmed and unfazed. The soldier uppercuts him, jabs him three times, and finishes with a punch to his chest. The soldier stands there out of breath, but J-Nel gives him a furious expression.

The air around J-Nel gives off a sheen which indicates his kinetic bands are hard at work. He could feel the blows being brought on him, but the pain was greatly absorbed by his bands. If his bands keep a consistent green light, then he is safe to receive more attacks, but a red light will indicate the bands are close to its limit.

The soldier throws another punch, but J-Nel catches the fist and absorbs the kinetic force from the blow. He looks the soldier dead in the eye as he lands a counter punch to his chest. In this attack, he sends out a measured amount of kinetic force he has absorbed. This results in a hole being blown through that soldier's chest.

The brass knuckles soldier looks down at the gaping hole as he falls backwards and dies.

J-Nel turns around to face the rest of his enemies. They are now more wary of him, but they keep their resolve. He takes four devices from the inside of his coat and throws them into the crowd, causing an explosion that instantly kills ten soldiers.

From their position, Christina and Karina can see and hear the explosion that J-Nel caused. They look at one another before running full speed in that direction.. With Karina's nanites and Christina's power, they are both running at thirty-five miles an hour.

Now that he has a free hand, J-Nel pulls out another laser sword and goes to work on his enemies. He sprints forward while cutting down any soldier that gets in his way. He plants his foot on a soldier's face so he can use that momentum to jump higher.

Afterwards, he takes that opportunity to dismiss one of his laser swords and throws four small explosives that take out a group of soldiers. He lands on his feet as he revives his previously dismissed sword. He dashes forward and slashes two soldiers in half.

A soldier lunges at J-Nel from behind, but he ducks while having both swords up. The soldier ends up flying over them and is sliced into four pieces.

Another soldier wielding a pair of Kuzuri weapons dashes in and slashes J-Nel across the side of his torso. He yells out in pain as he glares at the wannabe Wolverine fighter. He doesn't know how the soldier penetrated the protection of his kinetic field, but J-Nel will not let this transgression slide.

The Kuzuri soldier dashes at him again, but J-Nel is ready for him. He holsters one of his swords, then uses his free hand to throw a fist full of small balls onto the ground at the soldier's feet.

The soldier attempts to slow down, but it's too late. The balls create small explosions that knock the soldier off balance and sends him stumbling.

J-Nel rushes him and plunges his laser sword through the soldier's rib cage. He slices off one of the soldier's legs and brings the sword up to slice the soldier's head in half.

J-Nel breathes hard from the exertion and takes a moment to collect himself. He rushes forward to join Vyncent as they hold their own against this small army.

Vyncent is now breathing hard as he says, "This is more than we bargained for."

J-Nel grunts his agreement. He appraises Vyncent and notices he has accumulated many bruises and cuts from his own battles. J-Nel focuses back on their enemies.

"I'll admit, Vyncent, you have proven yourself today. I won't be mad if I die by your side."

Vyncent smiles as he stares at the odds against them.

Before he could form a reply, two daggers whip through the air to penetrate the heads of eight soldiers that were surrounding them.

J-Nel and Vyncent grin as a flurry of energy blasts rains down on the soldiers in the boys' close perimeter.

Karina and Christina leap into the air and land next to the boys with grace as they shift into their respective fighting stances. Christina's daggers materialize in her hands. No one speaks, but they understand it's do or die right now.

An explosion occurs that destroys the entrance of the duplicated SAGA doors. They all look towards the destruction to see Czar walking in their direction. It doesn't escape their notice that he is dragging Timulus behind him by his leg. He is unconscious.

Once he reaches the bridge, the soldiers create a path so there is a clear view of Czar. He lets go of Timulus and stares the humans down. He is no longer giving a grin, but instead an angry and annoyed expression.

"This ends now," Czar says menacingly.

Karina, Christina, Vyncent, and J-Nel look at him defiantly and with unshaken determination.

Czar takes note of their resolve and dashes into their direction.

The four also run towards him as well with their combined war cries.

Before these groups can meet, a pillar of fire erupts out of nowhere that makes everyone stop dead in their tracks. The pillar stretches from the ground as high as fifty feet into the air. Scorch marks spread and widen on the concrete, blackening the bridge into a shade of charcoal. The pillar spirals wildly and gives off so much heat that everyone in the area begins to sweat and struggle to breathe.

Czar guards his face while keeping an eye on what is happening, his curiosity evident.

The group looks intrigued, but they also use this moment to catch their breath as best they can.

The pillar narrows and shortens until it begins to take on a humanoid shape. The flaming fist reaches out and sends out an energy blast that kills fifteen soldiers. The fire pillar slows its wild surge and calms down to embers as a man begins to emerge from the dying inferno. A sunburst orange aura glows brightly as the man slowly descends to the ground.

Debris floats around him.

Fire dances around his muscles.

Golden light circles the air around him in a way that most would say only happens around a demi-god.

Streaks of fire shoot out from the figure and kill twenty soldiers in one sweep. A golden wave of energy launches forward from his hands that kills another twenty soldiers.

J-Nel's eyes widen as recognition sinks in. His mouth falls open as he drops his gun and clutches at his chest. He mumbles to himself incoherently.

Karina's eyes swell with burning tears as she places a gentle hand on her mouth. Not believing what she sees, she puts her other hand on Vyncent's arm to assure herself that she's not hallucinating.

Vyncent is too caught up in his own emotions to register that Karina is touching him. Like J-Nel, his mouth is also agape as he stares at the scene before him. He clenches his fist so tight that he can feel his fingernails breaking his skin.

Everyone can see a clear image of what stands before them. A bare-chested man with pronounced muscles wearing nothing but a pair of tattered pants. Intricate tattoos that resemble hieroglyphs begin on his shoulders spread down to his chest. His eyes are fierce with golden hazel eyes. His hair sways with the energy he is projecting. He stands with his back to the humans on the bridge. Desmond stands there with a golden aura that moves chaotically, but also with an angelic grace.

Desmond stares Czar down and exerts pressure that causes a tremor to be felt throughout the ground. He speaks with a calm tone in his voice.

"I told you before, Czar. I'm just getting started."

Czar stands straighter and flares his aura. It pales in comparison to what Desmond just showcased.

Desmond pivots his head towards his friends, but he makes eye contact with Christina first who responds by twirling her daggers with excitement.

"Alright, we have a newcomer. I don't know why you guys froze up, but don't sweat it. I'll take this guy out."

Everyone looks at her and shouts in unison, "No!"

She looks back at them in confusion.

J-Nel clears his throat and explains.

"That's Desmond. The friend we thought was dead."

Christina remembers what her mother said about him. She looks him over with new eyes.

He grins.

"Sorry I'm late, guys. I'm very proud of how much you've strengthened yourselves."

He looks back to Czar with a hostile expression.

"Let's finish this together."

The air around Desmond slows as he hears an old, yet strong voice in his head.

Show them who you are.

Desmond nods his head, and immediately jets off towards Czar with embers trailing after him.

Czar takes the cue and dashes towards Desmond as well.

As soon as their fists meet, a violent burst of wind moves through the onlookers. Desmond breaks the stalemate first by punching Czar with his other fist, but Czar maintains his balance and punches Desmond right back. For the time being, they slug each other with so much force, that the sounds of their blows are deafening.

Czar phases away, but Desmond's eyes flash as he turns and punches the air. Czar reappears only to collide with Desmond's fist. His fist glows brightly as he fires off an energy blast that sends Czar flying. Desmond chases after him and closes the distance.

Desmond reaches for Czar, but Czar wraps his tail around Desmond's wrist to fling him away. Czar's aura deepens as he opens his palms to fire a wave of energy at Desmond.

Desmond rebalances himself and dodges the energy wave, countering with a wave of his own. It completely misses Czar.

Czar grins at Desmond, but a shadow passes over him as another wave of energy collides with him from behind. A jolt of fiery energy surges through Czar's body as he screams in pain.

Desmond uses this opportunity to aim both his fists and fires a huge blast at Czar's face that sends him hurtling through the replica SAGA building.

The fighting on the bridge has stopped. It seems they all have forgotten to be enemies so they can watch this battle of titans.

Desmond hovers in the air as he stares into the direction that Czar landed. The ground begins to tremble. An aggravated shout can be heard.

Czar bursts through the debris of the building and stretches his hands out to his sides. He glares at Desmond with rage.

"You think you can win? Think again, human! I learned this from your precious master!"

Every surviving Plutonian soldier begins to glow with their own auras without the assistance of their Soul Packs. Each one in turn looks themselves over in awe at the power coursing through their veins. That is until some of them begin to scream in agony.

One soldier screeches, "What's happening?"

He immediately stops screaming and falls face-first to the ground. Other soldiers around him follow suit with the same fate.

Desmond understands what is happening, so he charges at Czar to stop him. While speeding towards him, Desmond spins rapidly until he is within reaching distance as he swings a kick at Czar's head. Czar catches his ankle. Desmond looks surprised by the strength in his grip.

"The sweetest part about this technique, is I can keep fighting while draining every one of them. Round two is now in session," Czar says with smugness.

Czar slings Desmond towards the ground, but he reorientates himself with ease. Czar dashes his way

Desmond clenches his fist as his flames become more prominent around his chest and upper arms. His body slightly trembles, but he doesn't take his eyes off Czar.

"A little fire is not enough to scare me!" Czar shouts with confidence.

It doesn't escape Czar's notice that the closer he gets, the thinner the air gets. His body is even starting to feel sluggish, but he decides to push through. He will not let this human win today.

Once Czar is mere inches away, Desmond flicks his wrist. A wave of fire erupts beneath Czar that consumes his entire body. Desmond shifts to the side to allow Czar's sprawling body to pass by him.

Czar immediately starts patting himself down as he screams at the top of his lungs. He's so furious that he begins cursing Desmond in the Plutonian language.

Desmond watches closely to see what this technique will do to him. Czar summons his aura and flares it violently enough that the flames dissipate. He has noticeable second degree burns on his chest, left thigh, right forearm, and random areas on his face. He breathes hard with exhaustion as he faces Desmond.

"I should've drained them all instead of saving the other half for your friends," Czar says with irritation.

Desmond raises an eyebrow to that. He sees a bright light in the corner of his vision. He looks towards the bridge to see that half of the soldier's remaining are being drained of their energy. The energy is being pulled into a specific area. At first, it was gathering into the shape of an orb, but now it is becoming humanoid.

Desmond's eyes widen as he understands what Czar really meant. Not only did he give himself a power up, but he also managed to create a new lifeform from the stolen energy.

This is a twisted lifeform though.

Berengia created Timulus from the lingering energy of dead allies. Czar, on the other hand, has forcibly taken this energy, and there is a chance that this thing will be more trouble for his friends.

Before Desmond can move to go help, Czar appears in front of him.

"Your fight is with me!"

Czar's aura flares as he aims a fist and blasts Desmond directly on the chest, sending him flying further away from his friends. Czar chases after him with a crazed and gleeful expression.

On the bridge, the energy has finished taking form.

Christina takes a step forward with a dagger in each hand.

"I've witnessed more unusual things around you people these past days than I have my entire life. Your friend is out there giving it his all, so let's work together so he doesn't think he has to worry about us."

Everyone else nods their agreement and steps forward to join her.

The blue energy slowly morphs into a dark shade of red. Its eyes glow with an eerie bright white light. It stands seven feet tall with a lean muscle body type and apparently is nothing but living energy. There is no flesh to be seen on this abomination. That brings to light a major problem. The group realizes it, and Karina is the first to voice it.

"That thing isn't good like Timulus at all. I'm sure we can hurt it, but it won't be easy."

"She's right," Christina adds. "I can sense that it only has one objective, and that is to kill us. We can either overpower it, or last long enough until it uses all its power."

Vyncent stares at the creature.

"How long could that take?"

As if it knew they were discussing it, the creature forms its aura, which in turn, also creates a gust of wind that slaps them all in the face.

Christina shields her face with her forearm.

"Judging from that show of force, who the hell knows."

The creature positions himself into a fighting stance and says only three words.

"I am Tsar."

J-Nel scoffs.

"Now that is the most self-absorbed creation I've ever heard of. Tsar and Czar is literally the same name."

Without hesitation, Vyncent dashes forward and lands a kick on Tsar's stomach. Tsar's body slides back with a hunched posture due to the blow. With a blank expression, he slowly lifts his head towards Vyncent.

Vyncent retracts his leg and spins to kick Tsar over the head with a loud crack.

Tsar stumbles to one knee, but he recovers and uppercuts Vyncent into the air. Tsar phases away and reappears in Vyncent's trajectory. He brings up both fists to knock Vyncent on his head to send him back towards the ground.

Before he makes contact, Karina floors her boosters at full throttle to catch Vyncent. She helps him to his feet as he staggers a bit.

A shadow passes over them.

They look up to see Tsar racing towards them fist first.

Two daggers materialize in front of them to block the attack and creating a stalemate. Nearby, Christina's pointer fingers are glowing while having them aimed in their direction. The force from the stalemate has her arms trembling with exertion.

Karina and Vyncent fly into the air and fire a blast of energy at Tsar's head. Their combined attacks create a cloud of smoke around him. The daggers whip around and slice away at their target. Within the smoke cloud, they can only see the sheen from the daggers making contact with Tsar. Christina does a hand gesture that causes her daggers to return to her. She catches them with ease and stands ready.

Everyone waits with anxious anticipation. The smoke slowly clears to reveal the state he is in. There are numerous cuts all over his body as well as two small holes through the side of his head and neck. Energy is rising like smoke from every open wound.

Everyone but Christina relaxes at the sight. Tsar slowly descends to the ground and seems to be staring off into the distance. His wounds close almost instantly with no sign of showing that he was attacked. The group tenses up with uncertainty.

Christina shouts out, "Don't be discouraged, our efforts are working! I can feel it's power waning!"

She didn't add that it was happening slowly.

Tsar looks down and notices five small balls rolling underneath him. The balls beep and a huge voltage of electricity shocks him into a paralyzed state. At least, it appeared that way.

Tsar's chest glows and a beam of energy is fired directly towards J-Nel. His eyes widen just before he taps the button on his belt buckle that summons the five-foot wide walled energy shield. The energy beam clashes with the shield, but only for a few seconds before the shield begins to crack. That gives J-Nel enough time to get out of the way before it shatters altogether.

Christina took advantage of the distraction and closes the distance as she initiates combat. Her eyes shine with her pale blue light as she does a running slide between Tsar's legs. After coming through the other side, she uses the momentum to kick off the ground and punch Tsar in the back of the head. She follows up by materializing her daggers and stabbing him four times in the back. She dismisses her daggers to grip his forearms and slam him headfirst to the ground. She tightens her grip to slam him a second time.

From his position on the ground, Tsar kicks her in the face, but Christina doesn't lose her grip. Instead, she feels emboldened as she slams him again and then throws him into the air.

Vyncent chases after him and punches him to the ground.

When he lands, Karina forms a long blade with her right hand and pins his hand. J-Nel joins in and pins the other hand with both of his laser swords. Christina manipulates her daggers to pin both of his ankles.

Vyncent aims carefully with a fist and fires a concentrated beam of energy at Tsar's head.

As soon as the attack happens, the others scatter away from the scene. Vyncent keeps up his energy output until he feels his body reaching its limit.

The smoke clears to reveal a headless Tsar. Before they can celebrate, the head slowly grows back as Tsar levitates to his feet. They all gaze in despair at the creature.

Tsar squats down and jumps in Vyncent's direction with incredible speed. Before Vyncent can react, Tsar punches him hard enough in the stomach to make him cough up blood. He follows up by elbowing Vyncent on the back of his neck that sends him diving to the ground.

Vyncent's aura dissipates, and he lies in his own body crater unconscious.

Tsar appears in front of Karina with his fist cocked and ready. Her nanite armor thickens around her face as he lands a punch that sends her skidding across the ground. After she stops rolling, the nanite armor uncurls from her face to reveal her unconscious state.

Tsar stands to his full height as he gazes at Christina and J-Nel without any emotion on his face. He opens his palms and lets loose a torrent of energy in their direction.

Christina readies her daggers just as J-Nel hovers his hand over the belt buckle.

A flash occurs between them and the energy wave as Timulus appears with his arms outstretched. The wave collides with his hands, and he strains to keep it in place. The force from the attack causes his feet to dig a few inches into the concrete and slide back.

Christina and J-Nel stare at him with disbelief.

Timulus grits his teeth and yells with determination as he keeps the attack at bay. His muscles bulge. Veins become more apparent on his arms and face, his aura flares with a fierce intensity, and his eyes are sketched with a deep resolve.

With a flash, Timulus and the energy wave both disappear. Tsar stands there with smoke rising from the palms of his hands.

J-Nel and Christina look at one another and back at Tsar. The air around them seems to electrify with an intense vibe.

A flash occurs directly above Tsar. He looks up to see Timulus and the previous energy wave diving straight for him. Without a second to react, they collide, and a huge explosion occurs in its wake.

J-Nel activates his belt buckle to protect them from incoming debris.

Minutes pass before the dust settles and they can see the silhouette of a body on the ground. J-Nel dismisses the force field to run over and check. Christina is right behind him.

Before they get too close, the figure slowly stands and turns to face them. They abruptly stop running. The figure takes a few steps to reveal it is Timulus. He appears to have cuts and bruises all over his body as if a semi-truck ran him over multiple times. They both let go of a breath they didn't realize they were holding. Timulus gives a weak smile.

"After I woke up and saw what you all were facing, I figured the best way to take it down was to use its own power against it."

Christina grins as she places a hand on his shoulder. He flinches due to the pain he's in, but he doesn't shrug her off. She looks him deep in the eye.

"I couldn't have done it better myself."

J-Nel gives him a nod of respect.

"Yeah, Timulus, way to show us up after we've been struggling with that thing."

Before any more words can be exchanged, Desmond's body flops onto the bridge and skids into their direction. His body stops a few feet away from them. He stands up and glares at Czar who is levitating in the air farther away. He turns his head towards Christina as he looks her up and down.

"Whoever you are, thank you for the help here. You seem very capable."

Christina eyes him with suspicion as she responds, "I do what I can."

Desmond focuses his attention back on Czar.

"I need to ask a favor. Continue keeping them safe."

Christina frowns at those words but Desmond continues.

"Even if that means from me."

Before anyone can question what he meant by that, Desmond plants his feet as he stares at the ground and slightly squats with his fist clenched. His golden aura flares to life as the tattoos glow right along with it. Desmond grits his teeth as veins bulge around his eyes and neck. The whites of his eyes turn dark gold, his nails sharpen into claws, his muscles harden with thicker flesh, golden energy forms on his back that slowly stretches out, and the hair on his head becomes thicker and wilder.

Timulus takes a step back and eyes Desmond.

"Desmond, was Berengia successful at making you a half demon?"

J-Nel and Christina look to him sharply and then back at Desmond to await his answer. The energy on his back has taken the form of a pair of wings. He speaks with a growl in his tone.

"No. I'm something far more dangerous than a demon."

He cuts his eyes upward at Czar and continues.

"Much more dangerous than a pitiful alien on a power trip!"

The energy wings flap once as they disperse to reveal dull grey, angel-like wings. The tattoos on his body glow consistently with a gold color as do his forearms, hands, and feet.

His wings flex outward at a span of four feet long and two and half feet wide. They flap once, which sends Desmond speeding towards Czar with godlike speed.

Desmond plunges both fists into Czar's stomach, but Czar refuses to allow this attack to send him off into the distance. Instead, he grabs Desmond's forearms to throw him aside, but Desmond doesn't budge. Desmond bends his body into a backbend to kick Czar in the face with both feet. This attack is successful at making Czar lose his grip on Desmond and hurl towards the ground. After landing on his back and creating a body print, he wonders just what is happening.

Before he can ponder further, Desmond lands feet first on Czar's chest and follows up with repeated stomps to Czar's body. The sound of bones cracking can be heard along with Czar's screams and spittle of blood gurgling from his mouth.

Czar makes a fist and fires a blast, but Desmond does a backflip to dodge the attack and lands a few feet away from him. Czar sits up and fires another blast, but one of Desmond's wings redirects it back at Czar. His eyes widen as he is hit with his own attack.

Desmond dashes forward and tackles Czar through the cloud of smoke. He digs his claws into Czar's chest. Czar punches him twice in the face, but Desmond refuses to relinquish his hold.

Desmond snarls as he slashes at Czar's face.

Czar manages to break free from him and jabs him four times. Czar connects the tip of his tail on Desmond's chest and fires a torrent of energy that sends Desmond spiraling. He lands on his back with smoke rising from his body.

Czar breathes with exhaustion as he stares at him.

"What the hell are you?"

The tattoos on Desmond fade away and his golden aura disperses. The others witness this with horror on their faces.

Desmond's body twitches as he begins to laugh uncontrollably. A familiar laugh that sends shivers down Timulus' spine.

The angel wings morph into a bat wing shape but keeps its grey coloring. His forearms, hands, and feet slowly adopt a grey color. A black aura erupts from his body as he levitates to his feet and stares at Czar with pitch black eyes.

Czar's eyes widen with recognition.

Dark King smiles at him, which in turn reveals the fangs in his mouth. He stretches and cracks his neck.

"Czar, we meet again. Don't worry, though. Unlike my vessel, I am experienced at handling overwhelming power. It's second nature to me. I have been itching to test drive this new power he has been gifted with."

By this point, Karina and Vyncent have recovered enough to watch the fight. Christina was able to fill them in on what happened while they were unconscious.

Dark King twitches his hands, but before he can make a move, Czar fires off two energy blasts at him.

Dark King grins with glee as one wing protects him. Instead of being deflected, the energy blast is absorbed into the wing. The other blast exits through the other wing and makes a direct hit on Czar's confused face.

Dark King rushes Czar and punches him in the stomach, following up with an uppercut that instantly bloodies Czar's mouth.

While soaring in the air, Dark King jumps up and elbows Czar back to the ground. Czar scrambles to his feet and throws a punch, but Dark King easily catches it and counters with a backhand. Dark King thrusts both fists into Czar's face and watches with a grin as his body skids along the ground.

"Lucky for you, this power isn't complete yet, or I would have finished you as soon as I awoke."

Czar fires another blast, but Dark King simply tilts his head to dodge it. This was only a distraction, though, Czar dashes in and throws a flurry of punches at him. Unfortunately, Dark King dodges his strikes with a slight chuckle.

"That's right, Czar! Give me your best so your death will be at its worst!"

Dark King parries Czar's punch and throws him a few feet away. His wings widen as black, needle-like projectiles shoot out and strike Czar relentlessly.

Dark King cuts his eyes at his right shoulder and notices there are sparks of energy that give him a slight muscle spasm. He ignores it for now and refocuses on his prey.

Czar keeps his guard up, but having delivered that attack is giving him hell.

Small, black swirling portals appear in front of each of Dark King's wings. The needle projectiles are now coming out of those instead. While Czar is distracted from blocking the attack, Dark King jumps high into the air like a rocket.

After a moment passes, Czar looks down and notices a shadow. He looks up only to see Dark King covered in a thick layer of black energy. He collides with Czar dead on. The needle attack abruptly stops as soon as they make contact. A loud boom is heard from the blow as well as a large cloud of dust. The others watch in amazement at the epic proportions of the battle.

Christina starts to speak, but a loud crack reverberates from the cloud of dust. Loud enough to make Vyncent flinch from the image he created in his mind. A loud thud and smack can be heard as well. After an eerie silence, a low groan can be heard followed by a painful welp.

Czar's body flies upward from the dust cloud, but it is clear to anyone looking that he was sent in that direction against his will.

Shortly after, Dark King takes flight after him and grips his arms.

Czar somehow still has a level of resolve enough to headbutt Dark King, which causes him to lose his grip. Czar lands a punch directly to Dark King's face and spin-kicks him towards the ground.

Dark King manages to land on one knee in a superhero pose. He looks at his right hand and notices it has sparks of energy coming from it now.

Czar breathes heavily as he stares Dark King down.

"Your punches are starting to feel weaker. Are you losing a grip on this new power of yours?"

Dark King mutters to himself as he stands up. He clenches his fist and glares at Czar.

If only there was a way to get over the limitations of this imperfect form, Dark King thinks. *That old fossil warned Desmond about this, but I didn't think it would be this bad. This power is becoming unstable.*

Dark King's breath catches, but he doesn't allow Czar to see the pain he's in. By using his peripheral vision, Dark King can see that sparks of energy are coming off his chest. The sparks are in such small patches they're hardly noticable.

The muscle spasms are annoying for Dark King, though, and he begins to feel a tingle on his spine that he wishes wasn't there at all. He does his best to ignore it.

He takes off into the air to engage Czar. In mid-flight, another muscle spasm happens on both of his thighs; again, he ignores it. He cross punches Czar and follows up with multiple jabs in the stomach. He spins around and kicks him in the head.

Czar retaliates by firing an energy blast, but Dark King dodges it and fires one of his own at Czar's chest. This creates distance between them and they have a stare off.

"You're too fast for me to connect a blow, but for some reason, you're not strong enough to deal enough damage to me to make your attacks worth it," Czar says.

Dark King's eye twitches at this proclamation.

Czar notices and becomes more confident with his assessment.

"It looks like all I need to do is wait until you don't have the energy to be so quick on your feet."

The tingle sensation returns. With a sigh of frustration, he mentally screams, *What?"*

Czar sees Dark King squint his eyes as if he's listening for something. Not knowing what to make of this, Czar decides to use the moment to allow his energy to replenish. Just as he begins a breathing exercise, he hears Dark King speak aloud.

"Fine, but just this once. After that, it's business as usual."

Czar just stares at him as if he's gone mad.

Dark King's black aura flares with an intense ferocity as a dome of silver energy surrounds his body.

Czar's eyes widen as he fires off multiple energy blasts at the dome, but they have no effect. He rushes forward to throw a flurry of punches at it, but that also has no effect. Czar reinforces his fist with his Spirit Energy and throws two strong punches at it, but this too has no effect on the dome. He stares at it with disbelief until he looks at Dark King who is projecting an unusual power.

Inside the dome, Dark King is gritting his teeth so hard that blood is leaking from his mouth. He is clutching his fist tightly enough that blood is dripping from his hands. He looks at Czar to reveal his left eye is pitch black and his right eye is now golden. Both are projecting an immense amount of energy.

His right wing morphs into a dull, yellow, angel-like wing. The same coloring consumes his right hand, forearm, foot, and the right side of the chest. The left side of the body remains as it was with Dark King's form. His body now has a dark orange aura.

Czar looks at this new development with astonishment. He looks down and sees that the palm of Dark King's left hand has the Oblivion symbol, but the top of his right hand below the knuckles has the symbol of something Czar knows very well. That particular symbol glows brightly.

"How did you do it human? How did you acquire the power of Hurak?"

Without gracing Czar with an answer, he smirks.

"You can call me, Void."

The dome breaks and bursts into specks of light. Void rushes forward and places both palms on Czar's chest to fire a wave of dark orange energy that completely consumes his body. Czar is knocked into the center of the rubble of what used to be the replica SAGA Headquarters. He slowly gets to his feet.

Void lands mere feet in front of him and growls.

"No more games, Czar. Let's finish this."

With a distained expression, Czar rolls his neck and flexes multiple muscles on his body. They dash at each other and face off. They attack with such speed and efficiency that their attacks connect in unison.

Fist to fist.

Leg to leg.

Forehead to forehead.

Everyone witnessing this battle is having a hard time keeping up with their movements.

Czar fires an energy blast, but the angel-like wing reaches out and halts the blast with its tip, directs it into the bat wing, and a small portal opens behind Czar that directs the blast at Czar's back.

Czar stumbles forward.

Void rushes him and clotheslines Czar to the ground. Without looking, Void reaches out his right hand and fires a wave of energy at him.

Czar rolls out of the way. He tackles Void to the ground and repeatedly punches him in the face.

Void uses both wings to smack Czar off him.

After landing on his feet a yard away, Czar dashes again at Void. Void stands ready, but Czar whips his tail around to fire a concentrated beam of energy that penetrates Void's left shoulder. He grunts in pain and staggers, but that's all the hesitation Czar needs as he follows up with a Spirit-Energy enforced punch to the head.

Void falls to the ground hard and scrambles to his feet to avoid a blow from Czar.

Void slaps himself and stares at his hand with an annoyed expression.

Void yells, "Don't tell me what to do, boy!"

He punches Czar and grabs his tail to throw him a few yards away.

Void continues, "If you listen more often, then you wouldn't be caught off guard, you asshole."

Everyone looks at Void as if he's gone insane.

Without continuing the fight, Void yells, "I have battle experience that your mind cannot comprehend! Do not think you have smarter battle sense than me!"

Void shakes his head.

"This has nothing to do with experience, just common sense. You're the one who underestimated his ability to recover from that last attack. Which I'll remind you, I said was a bad call!"

Timulus looks to his friends and explains.

"It appears that Desmond and Dark King have decided to combine consciousness to defeat Czar. Unfortunately, they can't trust each other enough to do efficient teamwork."

J-Nel stares at them and says sarcastically, "This day just keeps getting better and better."

Before Void can argue with himself further, Czar flares his aura and flies towards him.

Void becomes alert and dashes forward.

As soon as they collide, they lock each other's hands. Czar and Void glare at each other as they work to overpower the other with their own aura.

Timulus' eyes widen as he snaps his head in J-Nel's direction.

"Do you have enough power in your belt tech?"

J-Nel shakes his head.

"No, it only has two uses until it finishes the recharge."

Timulus then looks to Christina.

"I need to create a protective barrier, but I can't do it alone. I'm low on power-"

Christina interrupts him.

"Say less. Take my hand."

They grasp hands and instantly a dome of energy surrounds them all. Timulus grits his teeth.

"Stay focused, Christina. This is going to be intense."

A sphere of energy surrounds Czar and Void as their auras battle for dominance. Czar's eyes become mad with rage.

"You won't win this human. I am more in depth with my power, and you still struggle to understand what you can do."

Void doesn't respond, but instead allows his power to speak for itself. Their auras begin to mix and grow with overwhelming clashing. Above them, the sky darkens as a thunderstorm rumbles to life. Both Czar and Void's arms tremble as they fight to overcome the other.

Their energies collide and cause a violent torrent that spirals around them to the point that their bodies are no longer visible to the others. The energy from their standoff flows throughout the area so fiercely that it clashes with the protective dome.

Christina and Timulus struggle to keep the dome intact. The energy from the clash becomes so strong that it creates a blinding light and a gradual eruption of sound. A large explosion occurs from their position that sends a shockwave of energy to travel across the entirety of the replica island.

The protective dome from the group cracks, but it stands strong as they struggle to stay on their feet. The ground trembles and shakes violently.

After minutes of apocalyptic, Earth-trembling noises, the blinding light subsides, and the others look on to see what the result is. The protective dome has been shattered.

A chill runs down their spines as they hear Czar laughing with triumph. He laughs so uncontrollably that the others think it will haunt their dreams. Czar lies on the ground with a missing left leg and right leg. His left eye is closed shut and the rest of his body has unmistakable burn wounds, but he is alive. He lays there on his back, staring at the sky with a smile on his face. He shouts to anyone who will listen.

"I won! You hear me, Father?! Now that he's dead, I'm coming for you, and I will rule! I am the strongest! I am the one to be feared! I cannot be defeated!"

He continues to laugh hysterically, but his glee is cut short when a shadow passes over his face.

Desmond stands over him with glowing, golden pupils and energy streaking from his right hand in the shape of a blade. He is no longer Void. He has reverted to his original form.

Without any remarks, Desmond decapitates Czar with a quick and precise motion. Desmond breathes with exhaustion as he stares down at Czar. He dismisses the blade and unleashes a wave of energy from his palms that slowly disintegrates Czar's body to ashes. After feeling satisfied that the job is done, he collapses to his knees as he looks up to the sky.

Desmond starts to breathe heavily just before he screams loudly to release the pent-up stress he has endured. His screaming turns into a glorious war cry as his victory truly sinks in. He calms down and stares at his battered hands.

The group runs over and kneels to look at him with unexplainable respect.

J-Nel kneels to Desmond's level and reaches out a fist. Desmond looks at it and grins. Desmond bumps J-Nel's fist and they both follow up by tapping wrist to wrist and finish with a two-finger salute.

J-Nel speaks first, "You did it. It's over."

Desmond nods his head.

"For now, it is. Let's go home."

Everyone nods their agreement and looks towards the doorway. At the same time, they all notice that the doorway is much smaller than before.

On the other side, Rei and Skuzy sit on top of a mound of dead Plutonian soldiers. The SAGA agents stand on the bridge with horrified expressions due to the chaos they have endured today.

Berengia's energy form is sitting while facing the doorway with a pleased expression.

First, Christina and Timulus exit the doorway with J-Nel in tow.

Shortly after, Vyncent and Karina exit with Desmond's arms over their shoulders. Desmond is still conscious, but it is obvious he went through a hell of a fight.

Berengia stares at Desmond as he slowly rises to his feet. They immediately make eye contact.

"This part of the battle is over," Desmond says to Berengia.

Berengia nods his head in understanding, but he can feel foreboding dread.

As a unified team, they all head inside SAGA with proud expressions on their faces.

Behind them, the doorway shrinks even further until it completely disappears.

Mental Data Entry:

Eleven

I don't know about you, but I have been salivating ever since Desmond made his return. I stuttered for the better part of an hour trying to wrap my head around what was happening. His power, those eyes, and that specific type of flame. If Berengia hasn't figured it out by now, then he's a damn fool. I knew I was right to bet on that human. He's the prized horse I've been waiting for. His battle instincts have evolved so much that I fear they could almost rival my own. Almost. His companions have proven themselves as well. I have no choice but to keep my eyes on them. Especially that Jason fellow. He's just about as interesting as Desmond. Something about his blood makes me anxious. The lot of them are progressing further than I anticipated, and that could become a problem. I can't do much in this state I'm in, but soon I'll have to start creating some ripples.

Chapter Twenty-Three:
No Rest for the Mighty

Desmond is sitting up in a bed located in one of the medical wings of SAGA Headquarters. He is highly agitated. He knows the doctors are only carrying out orders from Kelly, but how many times does he have to tell them that he heals faster than any normal person. It's like they don't listen.

He thought if he showed off his power a little, the first doctor would back off. Instead, that doctor decided to bring three other doctors with him so they could help explains things to Desmond. It's amazing how they knew he could kill them without a second thought, but it was Kelly they were more afraid of.

He couldn't blame them, though.

As powerful as he is now, he's still cautious on how he speaks to her. Desmond has decided enough is enough. He is breaking out of this prison if it's the last thing he does. To hell with those self-righteous doctors. And to hell with anyone else who thinks they know what's best for him.

He gets out of bed and changes into an outfit J-Nel brought him earlier that morning. The outfit is his typical SAGA shirt and a pair of black jeans. He ties his boots on and stands up straight with a clear resolve.

Czar is definitely dead, but there are other threats out there waiting to show themselves. It's time to train and become even stronger, Desmond thinks.

Desmond briskly walks to the door and flings it wide open. Before he can savor the taste of freedom, he is unsettled that Kelly is already standing there. Her eyes are boring into his with an intensity that rivals any villain he's come across. He gulps loudly and opens his mouth, but no words come out. She stares at him unblinkingly.

"The doctors tell me you've been a stubborn patient as usual. Follow me."

Kelly turns and starts walking down the hall. Desmond immediately follows without question. They don't speak, until they enter the elevator. As soon as the doors close, Kelly sighs.

"I need you to know that you're not just a number, Desmond. It's been hard for me to come to terms with myself, but I do care for you. Therefore, I'm happy you survived, and I'm very proud of the man you have become. I've watched you grow from an adrenaline junky to a man who wants to protect rather than destroy. I've always known you were destined for great things."

Desmond stares at her and doesn't know how to respond. During his time at SAGA, Kelly has never worn her heart on her sleeve before. He feels moved by her words, but he is too shocked to say anything. Kelly cuts her eyes at him.

"Stop gawking at me like I'm a rare animal at a zoo. Come on."

The elevator doors open and Kelly exits without waiting for a reply from Desmond. He follows her, but he is still dumbfounded by their earlier conversation.

After a few minutes of walking, they enter a conference room where the others are waiting. This area is fitted with an oval table in the middle with leather chairs around it seating Vyncent, Karina, J-Nel, Christina, and Timulus. They all follow Kelly and Desmond with their eyes as they both make their way into their own seats at the table.

Kelly clears her throat.

"I'm sure you're wondering what this is all about."

Desmond looks around at everyone before he stares down at his hands.

"I'm sure I know. You all want to know what happened while I was away."

No one says anything.

Desmond looks up the ceiling and continues, "I guess I'll start at the beginning."

Chapter Twenty-Four: What Happened to Desmond

During the ceremony when Berengia was attempting to make Desmond a half-demon, something went terribly wrong. At least, that's how it looked to the untrained eye. What Berengia and Timulus were unable to understand is how the power coursing through Desmond wasn't destroying him. It was transforming his inner essence to mold it into its intended design. The demon strand that Berengia fed him was being absorbed rather than being bonded to.

After Berengia leaves, thinking him to be dead, a portal the size of a beach ball appears in front of Desmond's charred body. A cardinal bird flies out of it and hovers with an excited chirp above Desmond. It is the same cardinal Desmond has seen before.

The bird flaps its wings to send some of the ashes into the portal. It increases its flapping to break apart Desmond's corpse into more ash, which is now flowing into the portal at a rapid pace. Once all of Desmond's remains are inside, the bird flies into the portal and it closes.

The other end of the portal appears in a room seemingly surrounded by magma. Desmond's ashes burst through and begin spiraling in the air like a funneled torrent as they exit the portal.

Starting with his feet and up, his body begins to slowly reconstruct. Once it has finished replicating his skeletal form, organs are reconstructed, then muscle, and lastly his skin and hair. His body carefully lowers him to his back on the ground.

The cardinal bird lands on a rock a few feet away from him and chirps.

Desmond wakes up in a panic and sits up. He screams, but he stops because he can't remember why he's screaming to begin with.

He looks around with confusion. He's in a room. At least, he thinks he's in a room. The ceiling and walls look to be made of molten lava, but the floor seems to be made of pure gold. He stands up to examine further until he notices the bird. It chirps with slight amusement that he has finally noticed her.

"You're an interesting creature. I feel like I've seen you before," Desmond says with a suspicious expression.

He walks over to touch the wall, but a barrier becomes visible that stops him from doing so. The ground slightly rumbles as a chair made of gold rises from one end of the room. He walks over to it and examines it. An old, yet commanding voice speaks out.

"You may want to have a seat. When mortals gaze upon me for the first time, it can be extremely overwhelming for the mind."

Desmond crosses his arms with an amused expression.

"I doubt you can be more surprising than what I've been experiencing so far."

A brief silence occurs before the voice replies.

"As you wish."

A bright light appears in front of Desmond. A form is silhouetted within it. A pair of flaming wings stretches out from the light looking to be at least seven feet in length. After protruding out of the light, the wings expand to four feet in width. The wings flap once to shake off the roaring flames to reveal that they're made of gold. A being slowly steps out of the light with a humanoid shape.

Its skin is dark gold with Egyptian tribal markings on both forearms and hands. They're not tattoos, however. It's as if the markings were carved into the skin, giving those areas a stone-looking texture.

This being is bare-chested with golden bands wrapped around his biceps and a gold Usekh collar with intricate designs. From the waist to just above the knees hangs a black shendyt. It appears to be made of the finest linen Desmond has ever seen. Not to mention the decorative belt that consist of many different jewels containing various colors.

What really surprises Desmond is that he sees the body of a man, but he also sees the head of a falcon. The head has a golden beak and black feathers. The feathers near the neckline have embers on the tips. Its eyes are a golden hazel.

Desmond looks at its chest to find the symbol of a sun disk with a snake wrapped around the outer layer. This too doesn't look like a tattoo, but something else carved into its skin with an orange outline. This being has thick muscles that rival the most intense body builder and a neck thick enough that one would wonder if anything can cut through it.

The light slowly dims as a ten foot tall being stands in front of Desmond. During this entrance, Desmond has been staring unblinkingly. When he speaks, it is in a whisper.

"I didn't take my schooling too seriously, but I would recognize you from the many times I stared at your different depictions. I wrote a thesis about you. Your name alone carried a respectful weight during your time."

Desmond's knees begin to wobble as he continues.

"You're... you're the Sun God... The Sun God Ra."

Around Desmond's right eye, a tattoo slowly forms into the shape of the Eye of Ra. The tattoo glows gold just as Desmond slowly lowers himself into the chair.

"Well damn."

He passes out from the overwhelming force of Ra's power and collapses into a chair. The tattoo fades as the cardinal flies over and perches on top of the chair with an enthusiastic chirp. The right pupil of the cardinal flashes with the Eye of Ra as well.

Ra looks to his companion. He grunts with frustration.

"I don't see your obsession with this one. Look at him."

Desmond is now collapsed in the chair, completely naked.

An unknown amount of time passes before Desmond finally wakes up. He first notices the deity that is hovering across the room with his arms folded and aggravation etched all over his posture. His stare is so intense, that Desmond can feel him examining the depths of his soul.

Desmond notices that he suddenly has on pants, but nothing else. He thinks better than to ask for more clothes and instead makes a show of standing with confidence.

Within the recesses of his mind, he can hear Ra communicating with him.

"Desmond King, you are the first human in my bloodline to activate the Mark of Ra. A congratulations is in order, it seems."

When Desmond doesn't respond, Ra continues.

"Time exists differently in my realm. I can view many timelines, but because you beings have free will, there tend to be fluctuations. Now that you bear my mark, I will ensure you can wield my power without embarrassing the reputation of Ra's Flame."

Desmond shakes himself from his stunned expression and dumbly asks, "Wait. I'm actually related to you?"

Ra looks as if he wants to roll his eyes, but he refrains from doing so. Instead, he sarcastically responds.

"I bet you're considered a genius among your people."

Desmond looks taken aback by his comment.

"You're a god with a smart mouth. Got it."

Ra sighs deeply.

"Please Desmond, don't refer to me as that. Unlike the others, I accepted what I am over a millennia ago. Now, let's gauge where you are currently with your strength. Your power should be on a different scale since you went through a rebirth. Come at me and don't hold back."

Desmond hesitates because there's no way he can be serious. This deity, this Idol, is about as old as the world itself and he wants Desmond to attack him. For what? To demonstrate how much more superior he is? Well, Desmond figures if he's going to die today, then at least it will happen in the greatest glory he could have ever imagined.

Desmond's blue aura comes to life as he readies himself into a fighting stance. Out of sheer nervousness, a bead of sweat slides from his forehead down his neck. Desmond's muscles flex just before he charges forward with a fist blazing with Spirit Energy.

Without hesitation, Ra's right wing moves quicker than the crack of a whip with a blurred motion. Desmond's attack is halted as he stands in place with a disbelieving expression. He coughs up blood as he looks down with wide eyes.

The tip of Ra's wing not only penetrated the left side of his rib cage, but it also went straight through his back. He looks back up at Ra with horrified eyes.

"Do you always attack so wildly that you don't think to anticipate your opponents?" Ra asks with mild annoyance.

Desmond fully understands now that this sun god is in a league of his own, but he refuses to give up now. His eyes harden as he flares his Spirit Energy and looks at

Ra with a deep resolve. Ra's eyes narrow as he recognizes Desmond's determined expression.

Desmond brings his fist up to pound on the wing, but Ra retracts it and releases an aura of his own. Ignoring the blinding essence of the aura, Desmond jumps into action while yelling a war cry.

Ra audibly sighs with boredom as he uses his right wing to slap Desmond to the other side of the room. The wing slap also had a burst of flame that ignited against Desmond's face.

He hits the lava barrier back first and falls to the ground on his face. With much effort, Desmond positions himself on his hands and knees as he stares at the blood pooling beneath him.

"Don't be so dramatic. You're not going to die," Ra says impatiently.

Desmond doesn't hear him, though. His aura dissipates as he passes out.

Sometime later, Desmond awakens and wonders if his recent memories were just a dream. He manages to sit upright and sees the deity is still across from him. With a groan, Desmond rubs the back of his neck as he casts his eyes towards the floor.

"There are a lot of things you need to understand," Ra says with authority. "Your presence here has only one purpose. To guide you into using your power properly. I'm not completely all knowing, but I know enough to be confident you will do good in the Spectrum."

Desmond snaps his head up.

"Yes," Ra says with an impatient tone. "I know all about the Spectrum and the trouble it's in. I've lived long enough to rival hundreds of your lifetimes. The fool who encouraged you to become part demon doesn't know what he's doing. The way he forced your Potential out could have damaged your core and your power."

Ra retracts his wings and levitates in the air with his legs folded Indian style.

"Potential was meant to be bonded peacefully and in sync with the host body. If one can bring it out naturally, then that person can reach heights much faster than someone who was forced."

Ra shakes his head.

"A demon's essence is also definitely not the way to advance. Limitless Potential is not tied to such foul bloodlines, but we'll get to that later. First, what you have witnessed with Berengia is a form of mastered Potential. To the ignorant, he would appear to be close to being limitless."

Desmond shuffles to his feet.

"Wait, are you about to tell me that Spirit Energy started with you? And why are you calling it Potential?"

Ra closes his eyes for a brief second before he refocuses back on Desmond.

"No, it didn't start with me. What you know as 'Spirit Energy' predates life itself. It flowed freely when the universe was created. Not this mutated version you know as the Spectrum, but back when things were simple and pure. When beings came into existence that could sense it, the force was merely known as 'Potential.' The only desire this force had was to spread and share its essence with anyone who would use it for good. It was a giving power that wanted nothing more than to make a difference. Unlike its counterpart."

Desmond listens intently to this new information.

"You've seen it in action. The red energy that Czar uses is a perverse twin of Potential. It seeks out those who only seek ruin or exhibit destructive traits. In this age, beings are referring to it as Demonic Energy since mostly demons or other worldly creatures use it. In my time, we simply called it Rage. Rage was unable to bond with humans, and no one could explain why. I found it odd since there are plenty of destructive humans out there. The theory is that they manifested at the same time the universe was created, and Potential wanted to shield humanity from what Rage represented. That theory hasn't been proven yet."

Ra exhales deeply from all the explaining he's doing.

"Let's get back on track. There were many tiers of Potential, but only three of them truly stood out. The third strongest form was known as Paladin Potential. This form would be an example of where your power currently lies."

Desmond looks visibly surprised by this notion. He knew he had gotten stronger, but he never imagined being in the top three percentile.

"The second tier was known as Supreme Potential. This form is something that Berengia has showcased to you. And after you defeat Czar, you will face his father who also possesses this form. He already had an exceptional level of his own natural power, but adding Potential to the equation has elevated him greatly. You see, when someone gains access to Potential and they have an evil heart, it morphs into Rage."

Even though Ra can manipulate the temperature in his domain, Desmond has begun sweating from a sense of despair.

"What's important about these two tiers is that they have barriers, so to speak. In a way you would understand, the forms simply have limits. For most, the Supreme Potential tier is the highest to be reached, but even those forms take work to reach those limits. Berengia, Czar and Montezuma have yet to reach those boundaries.

"Now, tier one is an entirely different matter. To reach this tier, you must break through the limitations of Supreme Potential to reach Sacred Potential. This is a form you are capable of reaching because of the bloodline you possess. This isn't to say that this tier can only be reached through your bloodline. No, there are many other bloodlines that can reach this height. Even unqualified bloodlines that train hard enough have a chance. A very small chance, but a chance, nonetheless.

"Sacred Potential is not an instant milestone to becoming the strongest. This tier simply means you have the ability to grow without reaching any limits, but even this form requires work and training. In the long run, it is quite worth the investment. As you can see from my position, I am what honing Sacred Potential looks like."

Ra says all this with pride in his tone.

"That is all the information I will share for now. Let's do something about your combat instincts before we move forward.

Before Desmond can ask a question, he notices a shimmer in the air next to his head. Without any warning, a stream of fire jets out and engulfs his face. He screams out in pain just before he uses his aura to kill the flames. He breathes heavily as he glares at the sun god.

He looks around and notices there are five areas with small shimmers. Hip to the game being played, he readies himself to dodge. Unfortunately, a stream of fire comes from behind and engulfs him. He collapses onto his hands and knees.

Ra looks down on him with impatience.

"It is a mercy that you have survived this long. Being in my domain makes it difficult to pick up on energies around you. Instead of relying on spiritual sense, focus on your environmental senses. Let natural forces compel you into action when your supernatural abilities become unreliable. This will continue until you can hone those unnurtured senses."

For Desmond, it seemed as if this trial lasted for an eternity. In reality, it took him a few days to get the hang of the environmental senses that Ra was teaching him. After that, it took him only half a day to really excel at it.

Once he felt satisfied, Ra moved onto the next course for Desmond to face.

Desmond stands with aching muscles, but his pride will not allow him to ask for a break.

Ra breaks the silence in the room.

"Now that you have become accustomed to your other senses, it is time to make you familiar with your true power."

Desmond quirks an eyebrow at that suggestion.

Ra continues.

"That blue aura of yours demonstrates your initial gate for Potential. A necessary step to grow into, but now it is time to activate your mark. Close your eyes and reach deep within. Look for a spark that is unfamiliar to you."

Desmond does as he is told, but he strains to feel what Ra wants him to discover. After an hour passes, Desmond slouches his shoulders and looks to Ra for help. He can feel Desmond's plea for help, so he obliges.

"There is a way to help bring your power to the surface, but I warn you that this process can be intense."

Desmond waves the warning away.

"It can't be worse than the memory of me burning to death. I'll do anything that'll help me protect everyone."

Before he can continue his proclamation, a glint flashes in Ra's eyes and a torrent of fire surges around Desmond. The flames intensify as it stretches out into a ring. The fire and embers are so consuming that he can't see beyond them.

Ra's voice rings out.

"If you cannot triumph this challenge, you will die."

Desmond is instantly startled by his words. He probably would have used caution before agreeing to this had he known it would become life or death.

A puddle of black sludge forms a few feet away from him. Desmond stands ready with nervousness. His eyes widen as he sees someone slowly rise from the center of it. After fully ascending from the pit, Desmond's resolve falters slightly.

Across from him, Dark King smiles with satisfaction as he flicks the black goo from his body.

"Well, fancy meeting you here. Face to face too," Dark King says with mock amusement.

"Ra!" Desmond shouts. "What's going on? How is this supposed to help me?"

"Isn't it obvious?" Dark King asks. "I'm here as a motivator to reach your new level. You see, if you don't succeed right here and right now, I will destroy you from within and use your body to spread chaos. Starting with your friends."

At that omission, Desmond clutches his fist and glares at Dark King with utmost fury.

"You can give me the stink eye all day, Desmond, but it doesn't change the fact that I will be able to control this new power better than you ever could. I think I'll start by peeling the flesh from Karina's pretty face. Maybe even have my way with her while I do it," Dark King says with a chuckle.

Desmond has heard enough. He rushes Dark King with a determined expression, but Dark King simply phases away and reappears behind him.

Dark King now looks serious as he reaches his palm out towards Desmond to reveal his Oblivion symbol. The fire around them gives his pitch-black eyes a menacing glint. Dark King's face becomes serious before he speaks next.

"Begone."

Chaotic energy spirals around his hand as it flows towards his palm. Without giving Desmond a moment to think, Dark King fires a thick beam of black energy at him. Desmond brings his hands up to halt the attack with trembling arms.

"How long do you think you can keep that up? You stand there struggling, while I, on the other hand, can keep this up all day," Dark King gloats.

With closed eyes, Desmond's friends flash in his mind. He imagines what could happen if they faced Czar without him. He took in a vision of his friends being killed one by one with no regard for their lives. He even imagined Berengia doing nothing, since he is useless in that energy form of his. He pictures Dark King getting to them before they could even plan an attack on Czar, and that, for whatever reason, infuriated him more.

Desmond's muscles bulge slightly as veins become visible on his forehead and neck. He snaps his eyes open and stares at the smug grin on Dark King's face. His eyes flash with a dull gold color and a streak of flame exits from the inferno around them.

The streak circles him for a moment, until it makes contact and trails over Desmond's body. The heat from the flame strengthens Desmond and causes his trembling arms to stiffen. He takes a step forward as he grits his teeth.

Dark King is surprised by this, so he decides to use both hands to intensify his attack. The boost causes Desmond to flinch, but his resolve is set.

Starting at his feet, a golden aura flares to life. It travels upward until he is fully engulfed by it. His eyes shine bright with his new power, and he releases his own torrent of golden energy that penetrates Dark King's attack in half. Dark King's eyes widen as Desmond's attack consumes his entire body. Desmond relinquishes his energy and stands tall as he breathes from exhaustion. The ring of fire instantly vanishes, and Dark King's form withers away.

Ra stands in his place and looks to Desmond with pride.

"You have done well."

Desmond lowers his arms, but then he notices there are symbols and hieroglyphs that stretch from his shoulders and chest.

"Those markings will keep that dark presence in you from manifesting, but when you return to your world, that seal will have a time limit."

"Good to know," Desmond says.

Ra eyes Desmond before deciding something.

"There is more I need to teach you, but now, there is something I'm sure you're eager to know. I'm going to tell you the truth behind reaching Sacred Potential."

Chapter Twenty-Five: Where's the Proof?

The room is silent as they all focus on the story Desmond has been telling. Everyone looks at him with an intense expression. He looks up to finish his tale.

"From that point, he helped me to hone my new skills and transported me straight to the battlefield when you all needed me."

Timulus is the first to speak up.

"If you don't mind me asking, what did he say was the truth behind becoming limitless?"

Desmond shakes his head.

"I'm sorry, Timulus, but I'm not ready to talk about that. Honestly, I'm not sure I will be anytime soon."

"This is ridiculous," Christina snaps. "You really expect us to believe that an Egyptian god has been training you this whole time, and what, you're a demi-god now?"

"No," Desmond says simply. "I'm not a demi-god, but I am more than what I was before this experience. It's hard to explain."

Christina abruptly rises from her chair. Desmond does the same to accept whatever challenge she throws at him.

"Listen, Christina. I'm not a man who makes up stories and lies to the people he cares about. Everyone here can vouch for my intentions in life."

In response to what he said, everyone nods their heads in agreement. Christina walks around the table to face him, but Desmond refuses to back down. She narrows her eyes.

"Fine. We all saw what you're capable of, but I need you to show us something so grand that it is undeniable."

Christina jabs a finger to his chest. Desmond reacts and grabs her by the wrist. Instantly, they both warp out of existence.

Everyone else in the room immediately stands in concern and horror.

"What the hell just happened?" Karina asks.

Timulus looks around the room carefully and shifts his eyes towards the ceiling.

"I can't sense either one of them. It's like they literally vanished from our dimension."

J-Nel pounds a fist on the table.

"We just got him back! Damnit, when will this shit end?"

Chapter Twenty-Six:
Soul Ties

Desmond and Christina find themselves in a peculiar place. The best way to describe it is as if they are inside an aurora. Colors and rays of light are swirling with an elegant grace all around them. Desmond releases her wrist and gazes at the sight before them.

Christina looks at him with an accusatory glare.

"Ok, you made your point. Send us back."

Desmond snaps his head in her direction.

"I didn't do this. I thought your craziness was at work here."

They stare at one another as the truth sinks in. Christina moves to summon her daggers, but her power doesn't seem to work in this place. Likewise, Desmond reaches deep to form his aura, but he also discovers his power doesn't work. They look at each other with deepening concern.

A loud screech and roar can be heard in the distance. They both slowly move so they are standing back-to-back.

"I don't care what comes our way. We will survive this," Christina says with confidence.

Desmond nods in agreement.

First, without knowing what he's looking at, Desmond sees the Lazuli Dragon before him. A large and intimidating presence that demands respect. The Lazuli stares deep into his eyes as if daring him to look away, but he doesn't. He holds her gaze without flinching.

Behind him, Christina is looking at a fiery bird. Its massive wings call for admiration as it hovers before her. The gold eyes of the Blazed Bird draw her in like a lullaby.

The Lazuli and the Blazed Bird make eye contact. Desmond and Christina are now standing side by side as they witness these two entities come together and share their essence with each other. The azure and gold energies mingle with one another in a sense of harmony and love. A gentle breeze washes over them with those combined energies, causing them to look at one another with a question on their minds.

Before anyone can say anything, they both feel a tingle traveling through their bodies. Christina looks at her left inner wrist and notices a small patch of gold energy. It is faintly glowing, but she can feel an immersed connection tugging at her.

Desmond finds that the tip of his right index finger has a faint, pale blue light coming from it.

At the same time, they both realize that Desmond grabbed Christina's wrist with that same hand. They look at each other with bewilderment just before they warp out of existence once again.

Chapter Twenty-Seven:
I Need Answers

In the conference room, there are a team of scientists scanning the area with various devices and equipment by Kelly's orders.

Timulus is levitating in the center of the room, doing his best to find a trace of Desmond's energy. J-Nel is angrily pacing the room while also stopping to check the readouts the scientist has. Vyncent and Karina stand by the only window in the room to give each other silent comfort.

Timulus opens his eyes just as Desmond and Christina blink into existence before them.

Everyone stops what they're doing to stare at them. J-Nel moves to say something, but he stops short when he notices how intently the two are staring at each other.

Desmond's eyes are wild while Christina has a slight blush in her cheeks. Desmond shakes himself and looks around at everyone else.

"Don't worry. Everything is fine, but I need to go talk to Berengia," Desmond says with a hoarse voice.

"I can take you," Timulus offers.

Desmond puts out a hand to stop him.

"That's alright. I have my own way to get to him now. If you don't mind, I need to speak with him alone."

After a last, lingering glance at Christina, a tornado of fire engulfs Desmond for a brief second before he disappears altogether.

Vyncent whistles and says, "Wow, that's new."

Now everyone looks to Christina, who decides to stare at the floor without acknowledging them. There are so many thoughts rushing through her head, but she's not sure what to make of what she just experienced. She quickly flicks her wrist and aims her pointer fingers at a nearby wall to summon her Ka Gate. She all but runs into her entrance to the Lazuli village as it closes behind her in a flurry.

They all look at one another.

Kelly asks, "What's up with those two?"

Karina shakes her head with a grin.

"Who knows. Kelly, before you decided to call this meeting, you never answered my question. Now that Czar isn't a threat anymore, tell me where she is."

Before Kelly can respond, Sahar comes bursting into the room and breathes in the air dramatically. She is currently dressed in navy blue tights with a matching tank top that has SAGA etched in a corner. Her hair is styled in a double braid bun fashion with auburn coloring.

Karina studies her and takes in the fact that her muscles have toned nicely since the last time she saw her.

"Sahar," Karina says cautiously. "What happened to you? You're even walking around bare foot which is unsettling considering who you are."

Sahar chuckles at her words.

"Well, Kelly offered to put me and Javon in her secured facilities until Czar was dealt with. We accepted, of course, but I wanted more. When Czar had me chained up like some animal, I vowed to never be a damsel again. So, I asked Kelly for special training while I was locked away."

Kelly grunts to interject.

"More like demanded. Karina, she was absolutely determined to transform herself into a death machine."

"Why didn't you come to me?" Karina asks with a hurt tone.

Sahar brings her friend in for a hug.

"Because we all know how protective you all are of me, and I didn't want you guys to talk me out of it. The next time there's a battle, you guys can rest easy knowing that I can handle myself now."

Vyncent steps forward with a question of his own.

"Where's Javon?"

Sahar looks at Vyncent with a regretful grin.

"Javon had other ideas. He wanted to just run off to another country and forget all this supernatural business that came into our lives. We argued for weeks until he gave me an ultimatum. I leave with him so we can live peacefully, or he leaves without me to never see him again."

A brief silence occurs until she continues.

"As you can see, I'm still here. I wanted more and he wanted to run."

While they continue to converse, Timulus is looking at Sahar with new eyes. On one hand, he is moved by her passion and her having the strength to follow her own path. On the other more important hand, he notices something that no one else in the room can see.

Deep in Sahar's core, Timulus can see a power flowing within her. He can see how strong and beautiful it shines inside of her. He deduces that it's not Spirit Energy he's seeing, but something that is extremely rare in this part of the Spectrum. He has no doubt that when the time comes, she will blossom into a force to be reckoned with. Until the right time, he decides he will stay quiet regarding his findings and see who she becomes. There's no doubt in his mind that Berengia has already sensed her hidden power. He will make sure that she's not taken advantage of.

Timulus walks over to the group and places a firm hand on Sahar's shoulder. She looks to him with a warm expression, and he instantly knows he was right to assume that she will become great. He grins at her.

"Continue doing what you're doing. You're going to make your friends proud."

Meanwhile, Christina has been staring at her wrist for the last ten minutes. She simply doesn't understand why it is still glowing. She tries to cover it with the sleeve of her jacket, but that does nothing to rid her of it.

After a quick search, she finds her mother on a hillside gazing into the sky with a peaceful expression. She almost decides to leave her, but her mother senses her and uses a hand gesture to motion for her to join. She does.

Jade glances at Christina with a keen eye. Jade jumps to her feet and looks deep into Christina's eyes.

With a show of embarrassment, Christina says, "Mom, I could really use your help. Something happened."

Christina turns her hand over to reveal the fading light on her inner wrist. Jade examines it and looks back at her daughter with a smile.

"This is the mark of a Soul Tie," Jade says with glee.

Christina frowns.

"I didn't think there was a literal symbol, though."

Jade shakes her head to further explain.

"Normally our teachings suggest that two people who are meant for one another create a bond in mind and soul. The body is just superficial compared to the mark of the Soul Tie, but I'll be honest that it has never been documented to have a physical manifestation. If the mark is visible, it speaks volumes to your destiny with the other person. Desmond will make a fine son-in-law."

Jade gushes at the thought.

Christina snatches her hand away incredulously.

"Who said it was Desmond?"

Jade waves away her daughter's denial.

"Please, child, have you forgotten I am one of the Elders? I knew for a while that a possibility for a union existed between you two."

Christina stares at her mother in disbelief. She looks down and is relieved that her inner wrist has stopped glowing. At least now she can hide the evidence of her shame.

Meanwhile, Desmond has conjured himself at the Indigenous Bridge. He looks at the tip of his finger and is relieved that it has finally stopped glowing. He can now have this long overdue conversation without distraction.

As if sensing that Desmond is now focused, Berengia's energy form appears before him with a look of hesitation. They stare at each other for a long moment.

"I need to ask you something before we get into it," Desmond says plainly.

Berengia nods his head for him to continue.

"When you attempted to make me half-demon, were you absolutely sure I would survive? Or were you very aware that I had a chance at dying?"

The air around them becomes thick with tension. The only sound that can be heard is Desmond's breathing. All the while, Berengia maintains eye contact with him without a sign of wavering.

"Ever since I met you, I had a sense that you are meant for great things on this world and throughout the Spectrum. My confidence in you also subconsciously turned into arrogance. I allowed myself to believe that you can overcome anything that's thrown at you. So no, I didn't put you through that knowing it could fail, but I can admit I didn't allow myself to consider it either."

Desmond nods his head.

"Thank you for your honesty. From this moment forward, I want us to work together as equals. I can still learn from you, but at this point you can learn from me as well."

"I agree," Berengia says with a humble tone. "But can you confirm my suspicions? Was I correct to assume that you share qualities of a certain sun deity?"

Desmond hesitates for a moment. He just got Berengia to agree that they are equals, but for some reason he wasn't sure what he should share. He pushes away his doubt.

"Yes, you were correct, but my power isn't complete and demon blood wasn't the answer."

"Then what is the answer?" Berengia asks with curiosity he couldn't hide.

Desmond sighs.

"One day I'll tell you, but not until my power is complete so the proof is evident. For now, tell me what you can about Czar's father."

Chapter Twenty-Eight:
Joining the Fray

Later that night, a door to a small room opens for a man to walk inside. He closes the door and sits cross-legged on the floor. The room is dark and bare, with nothing but a tall mirror propped against a wall.

The man is shirtless, barefoot and wearing nothing but boxer briefs. The air inside the room is thick due to the fact that there isn't any air circulating. It's humid inside to the point that the man glistened with sweat just moments after entering.

He breathes deeply as he takes his body through familiar breathing exercises. His hands rest on his knees in a relaxed posture. He lets all the tension from his body flow out of him as he concentrates on his heartbeat and nothing else. His mind is clear without any stress to distract him.

He's been at this for a long time, but he'll be damned before he gives up now. The tendons in his neck jump with a slight spasm. He ignores the intrusion and continues his breathing exercise with patience.

He can feel sweat pouring down his face and body. If he wasn't so determined, he would allow himself to feel mortified by the sweat pooling beneath him.

His biceps twitch one at a time for three seconds each. His chest experiences a slight muscle spasm as if it's jealous that the rest of his body is going through something. His mind is locked in a trance so he can ignore the nagging irritation his body is enduring.

That is, until he feels something different. Whatever this feeling is, he knows this is what he has been waiting for. He's sure of it.

Tentatively, he slowly opens his eyes and is excited that the room has been filled with light. He uses his peripheral vision to see from the mirror's perspective that his eyes are giving off a dark green hue.

This is the first time he has manifested this power and he couldn't be more excited. It is just the eyes for now, but in time he's sure he can manifest his own aura with more practice.

J-Nel nods to his reflection and silently congratulates himself. He remembered Desmond saying that any living being had the potential to draw Spirit Energy out of themselves. He's been putting his body through a lot of these routines the past few weeks, but his hard work has been paying off. He thinks about his best friend and imagines what he would say.

J-Nel smiles to himself and calmly whispers, "I'm just getting started."

Epilogue

Mila and Kogi slowly back away as the prison pods light up and power to life. They both look so disheveled and unkept that anyone passing by would assume them to be homeless.

Montezuma forced them to work nonstop until they completed their task. They feel proud knowing they were able to do so without tempting Montezuma to kill any innocent Plutonians to motivate them. They couldn't believe they managed to solve Pluto's most protected secret. They look at each other and back at the pods. They slowly move to retreat, until their backs collide with Montezuma's form. They flinch in surprise and move to distance themselves from him.

Without looking at them he says, "I am grateful for your efforts. As a mercy, I will allow you two to leave now. I can't promise that I can protect you from them."

Mila and Kogi ran out of the lab without a second thought.

The lids of the pods slowly open to allow smoke to be released, but one of the lids is kicked open violently as a figure jumps out of it. He screams, curses and looks around madly for something to tear apart. Montezuma is in front of him in seconds to look deep in his eyes.

"Calm yourself, you are free now."

It takes the male Plutonian a moment to register who he is looking at. When he does, he instantly relaxes and bows to Montezuma.

Unlike other Plutonians, this male's skin is rough and jagged with an onyx complexion. His eyes are slightly smaller, and he has fangs in his mouth. He is dressed in rags that are torn all over and his hairstyle is black cornrows that stop at the base of his neck. His nails are sharp as claws and his eyes are a mix of yellow and pink.

From the other pod, another Plutonian climbs out and looks at the two with astonishment. Instead of waking in anger, this one has a calm, destructive demeanor about him. This male Plutonian, in contrast, has smooth skin with circular patterns all over his body. His complexion has a dull ivory hue that stands out in the population. His nails are neat and trimmed, while his eyes are bright silver. His hair is fiery red, straight, and long enough to reach his back. He is also dressed in rags. He walks closer to them and kneels next to the other newly freed Plutonian.

Montezuma looks to the one with the cornrows and says, "Omega." He looks to the other, "Alpha."

They both look up to meet his gaze. He places a hand on both of their heads as he releases a pulse of energy into them.

"Focus on the flow of power I am sharing with you and take it. Force the power to bond with you."

With complete obedience, they allow the surge of energy to consume them. Unlike everyone else who went through this process, these two take on the task without flinching in pain. Omega's nose begins to bleed, but he shows no signs of discomfort. Alpha, on the other hand, is smiling from the way the skin on his hand is bursting and healing immediately afterward.

Minutes pass before, Montezuma releases them and notions for them to rise. They stand up straight with their new red auras on full display. They grin at one another before turning their attention back to Montezuma.

"I know you are wondering what happened after Berengia locked you two away. Unfortunately, he won that day," Montezuma says with a grin.

Alpha and Omega frown at this news.

Montezuma continues, "Do you feel the new power that courses through your veins? Can you feel your natural abilities elevating to better heights? We now have the chance to finish what we started long ago. That lab-grown failure of a son couldn't pull his weight, but now that I have my real heirs with me, the universe will bend to our will."

The two sons smile at this proclamation.

"After you get reacquainted with your power, I will immediately send you two to Earth to hunt Berengia and his warrior down. He has bound me here by unknown means, but this war is far from over. We will triumph!"

Alpha and Omega raise a fist to him and yell in unison, "Yes, Father! We will show them true despair!"

Montezuma smiles wickedly.

While Montezuma is celebrating the freedom of his sons, there is another event happening on Pluto.

There are two male Plutonians descending a ladder that leads them into an underground tunnel. After reaching the bottom, they both stretch and groan from the long climb down. They raise their lanterns to illuminate a nearby wall to see a hieroglyph of a fiery bird. One of them walks closer to examine it.

His name is Nume. A short, muscular Plutonian with a shaved head.

The other is called Zor. He is a tall, lanky Plutonian with a braided top knot hairstyle. His hair color is a bright greenish blue.

While Nume examines the wall, Zor takes the opportunity to kneel on one knee as he places his right hand on his chest. With his eyes closed, he silently says a prayer.

"May our fallen brothers find peace in the afterlife."

Zor recalls his memory of watching his village fight to ensure their safety. He stands up and faces Nume.

"This is the easy part, brother. As the last appointed Sons of Ra, we have a duty to uncover the means of unlocking his power. Not just Pluto, but all life is depending on our success. We know the path. Now we must solve the puzzle."

Zor raises his lantern to reveal the long walk in the catacombs before them. Nume shifts his lantern to reveal another hieroglyph that is a variant depiction of the Blazed Bird. This hieroglyph illustrates the Blazed Bird in a humanoid form with a fist raised high accompanied by an aura surrounding his body and fist. Unlike the depiction of the Blazed Bird, the humanoid hieroglyph has the head of a man.

"Yes," Nume says with reverence. "We must free Ra's champion, Hurak."

Acknowledgements

I would like to thank my beta readers for the time they have put into combing through the rough draft. They are: Mandy Cook, Deandre Robinson, Keishaunda Haynes and Danny Raye. You all gave me great input and criticism. Without you, the book would not be in the great shape it is today.

I would also like to thank my beta readers for returning for the gamma phase. There are new names for this group as well. That includes, Joshua Cook, Shelby Coral, Keishaunda Haynes, Mandy Cook, Deandre Robinson, and Danny Raye.

A special thanks goes to Danny Raye. Along with being a beta reader, she also became my editor. She has been fundamental in making my book as great as it can be. You can find her on Fiverr. Her efforts go harder than any level up that Desmond achieves. Thank you Danny.

About The Author

Darius Knight lives in South Georgia. He found his love for writing during high school. For most of his life before that, writing was only a hobby to either make his friends laugh or to create tales for others to escape to. His dreams and his love for anime and gaming are what fuels his imagination. He created Knight Vision Stories to have an outlet to express his creative side. Follow his journey through his writing because his story doesn't end here.

Made in the USA
Middletown, DE
23 June 2024